The Maiden &
The Demon

An Urban Gothic
Romance

K.L. Miller

ISBN: 0615672442
ISBN-13: 978-0615672441

DEDICATION

From Start to Finish, this Book is dedicated to My Pack. Thank you all for sticking to this Old Wolf's side.

CONTENTS

ACKNOWLEDGMENTS

Thank you, God on High, for doing what few
Humans would: have Faith in a troubled Soul
traveling a lonely, dangerous road.

And with Arrogance and Rage

The Curse was cast

And the Maiden of the Deep

Heard

Chuckled

and Answered the Hideous Cry

Woe to the Child with Power

For from such Foolish Hearts

Come Tales of Suffering

25-8

"He looks like he's ready to kill someone."

Chica *really* needs to Understand: I hear whispers easily. Comes from my love of Music: listening to the subtle sub-harmonics and rhythms. And I'm **not** discounting my rampant Paranoia. It hears whispers where there are and aren't Sounds. I don't react, however, moving smoothly from cutting chicken to Plate Presentation, letting her enter my sight only when I spin to my left to see where Jo-Jo's at with the Appetizer for this Table. As usual, the *instant* my eyes slide over her body, she tenses. The Servers around her immediately throw glances towards the line, looking for me: **Demon.**

Everyone stops; a few high-pitched Girl-Squeals and OOooos swamp the Back Line. Amy's return from giving birth to a beautiful boy is Why: **mandatory** Girl Moment. I doubt anyone noticed the two nanosecond Stare-Down we had, since no one looked my way;

and they *always wondered* how I manage to disappear so quiet y, especially with the plethora of key chains dangling from my hip: **SHADOW SKILL.**

* * * *

"What if he were your Child?"

"I'd do Right by him; Words... and the Truth, but we'll never know, will we?"

"Why are you so cold to me?"

* * * *

"Whuddup D?"

"WHOOOOAAAAA!"

Feels good to Greet Kilo as he swaggers from the back dock, Newport stench not quite masking blueberry-blunt-of-Reggie. I prefer casual Street Greetings as they remind me of the Human within the Flesh; Kilo's greeting jerks me from the darkened memory. I jerk my head up, pure Street Warrior, as we make eye contact. My stride shifts from Workplace Grind to Pimp as Good Feelings swim through my muscles. If there is a Down-Side to the Warm Fuzzies, twisting a smile into the dead straight-line my lips threatened to turn into a sneer/snarl, it doesn't show up until after Chef, grinning wide (he **likes** seeing me Pimp-walk: reminds him of a Tale or three) lets his eyes drop from Happy Heights straight into *Watch Out* Mode; Cook's Warning: Management's got sand in its twat... *again.*

Note to anyone who cares to Know a bit about Behind-the-Scenes in the Restaurant Industry: Sex is a wicked double-edged dagger. I'm in hot water because I **didn't** Stick Dick in her. Now... every little slip-up becomes fuckin' Mt. Everest; only made WORSE because I'm Male. Yep... Sexist... and **married?** Hey... this is Biz, nothing Personal; been waiting for her to turn this against me for about six months.

"Desmond?"

I bite back my usual, "What's wrong now?" No sense in getting fired in the middle of an eyebrow deep Recession. But I don't drop Pimp, especially since she's Posted Up like a confident Corp Raider about to eat another Soul.

As I Pimp back into the Kitchen, cock-sure smile slipping from lips into my eyes, I spot Chef prepping one of the new dishes for tonight. He glances at me, shakes his head and makes **sure** she doesn't see the smirk on his face. Of course, with Ruthless Bitch banging at her Happy Mask, everyone is in Trouble. The Cooks don't blame me. They're covering their own elation.

"Bitch failed again?"

I toss the Jo-Jo a wink before heading to the dressing room and the private bathroom shared by the Cooks; needed Solace to Think.

* * * *

Rush; I'm Zero-Bubble like the other Cooks. Servers... well, they're putting up with Pissy Customers. And right on cue, She-witch pops in to Drop Shit. Only this time, it **is** Personal: someone in my Blood Family got Locked Up. The Cops were looking for me **at work!!!!!!!!** She didn't even bother to keep the Racist Look from her eyes and Stance. I didn't rise to the bait because there were Assassins looking for me.

"*Demon.*" I hear Chef; my reaction? I adjust the chef's knife in my right hand slightly. At that Moment, the only thing moving through me is Street Survival Instincts.

I step off the line just as two white cops slide around the corner. My ears pick up the sounds their shoes make on the Kitchen floor, along with their side-arms sliding slightly against Combat Fatigues. Like I said, **assassins**... right down to the dark shades meant to intimidate as well as keep Sharp Eyes like mine from boring into their Souls. It's easier to hide Fear when you're wearing Shades.

One is a Rookie; the instant his eyes spot my knife, his hands *tighten* on his side-arm, the clasp already free and clear. Fucker probably hasn't gotten his Nigga Notch yet, judging from how he works his Just-Past-Puberty clean-shaven jaw.

"Mr. Mathers, we are not here for you or to start anything." Sound odd?

Anderson knows me. He and three other Cops tried to 'insti l Respect' in me one day. Didn't work then, and he knows I have no Fear of them, God or Death. If Rookie decides to make this ugly, I've got no problems; Anderson *hates* unnecessary paperwork.

"Sir, put..."

"Hold it. Mathers, your cousin is in jail; he asked us to contact you about his alibi."

"***After the Rush; now...***" Rookie swells up; the entire Dish Crew finds a wall and posts up, all eyes watching the spot where hand-to-hand combat was sure to happen. That's where Chef appears, his back to me and *clear* in case I had to swing or use him as a Human Shield; knife to a gun fight, Knife Close the Distance. Fast.

As Chef starts talking, I size up Rookie. He can definitely hang in a fight, but he's trained to go up against Street Flailers and Slap Boxers... **not** a Trained, Skilled Killer. I slide easily into a stance, and right then his Fear goes from Red Alert to Action. I see him take in a small breath; his throat twitches as he prepares to Command with Voice.

"Officer, you'll have to shoot me to get to Demon," comes Chef's quiet voice. Everyone working draws in a deep, astonished breath. Rookie starts to say something when Anderson stops him with *his* Command Voice.

* * * *

"Why'd Chef call him Demon?"

"Yo... don't go askin' 'bout dat Nigga; he's O.G.; been Places... done Thangs."

I dive into my Work, fighting the cavalcade of Emotions ripping through me. Hate being In a Mood while trying to Make Money, especially Paranoia: it keeps turning over every Expression on the Manager's face before, during and after. I get a small Change: Amy was there with her newborn, but the Happy Moment is stabbed by painful Memories, and **more** Emotions rush in, darkening the Mood-horizon ominously.

"Fuckin' A..." I slam down on my Thoughts, filling my mind with frozen darkness beyond oblivion. I check around, looking for and spotting an opening. I'm Ghost before she can bring her child near me, headed straight for the Smoking Room.

The Men's Bathroom for Employees is located in the most obscure part of the place, and is well-ventilated. Before you fixate on the smell of Male Shit and Piss... its primary Use is for Tokin' Up; Li'l Mikey stands Security; he flips me a nod as I breeze by.

"Re-Up ya, bro," I mutter, **hard** Pimp in my Tone... and this surprises me slightly. I ponder this as I dodge one of the Dish Crew. We exchange Pounds (hand greetings) and he jerks his eyebrows up. I shake off the offer; got Grim with me, my One Hitter. Closing and locking the door, I take time to look at my face in the mirror... *really* look at me. Getting old and doing so as gracefully as Life will allow, I've got Gray Hairs here and there. They stand out (to me), each a Memory of some Stressful Moment. I frown slightly. My Goatee needs to be neatened-up as usual; I try not to think about the scruffy cheeks, mainly because of the Memory: Amy's hands *caressed* my scruff.

As I take a hit, I try not to chuckle into a cough. The **reason** I won't Stick Dick in the Manager is Amy; learned I don't like being Back Door Man because of her. The kid is her Ol' Man's (got the proof, though I doubt **he** knows she had the Test done; yeah, it was **that** close).

And I do **not** like the Role of Dick-in-the-Glass-Case: *platonic Friend.* Amy and I haven't spoken in some time, though she does check my Facebook page frequently.

I try not to wonder how she feels about me; hurts too fucking much to even **think** about her. Fucked Up and Fell-in-Love with her, and she allowed *me* to get too close; Never said Those Three Words, and I'm strangely grateful for that. She was looking for Fun and Kinky Sex, **not** someone her Heart found enticing.

Before I let the emotions overwhelm me I'm Thrice-Baked; five hits of Kush will do that. I allow Time for the fan to suck up any lingering smoke, cover the overpowering funk as best I can with the can of spray, then, after one last check in the mirror... head back.

"Where's Daddy?" *Perfect fuckin' timing, yo.*

* * * *

Manager is busy. This is a blessing, and here's Why: Amy comes into view holding her Child tenderly; our gazes meet...

*I really do Love her; pity shit didn't Work out. Not quite used to being Poison to a Female; **never** got used to Breaking Hearts either. Can't ignore the pained look deep in her eyes; too busy admiring the rigid Mask plastered to her face. Still wondering who if anyone knew about us. She doesn't even speak outright... just moves her lips; probably wants to call me McGruff.*

Pet Names; big no-no if the whole mess is as DL as I've checked it out to be. The only person capable of Snitching me out wants my dick too; Petty... but a First for me. She fixes her gaze just behind me; nice trick, except she's fighting locking gazes with me.

*If she's looking for the kind Lover she held, she's shit the fuck outta luck. Been Burned a few times since we split and really don't have it **in** me to give a shit about **anyone**. She's Collateral Damage, pure and Simple: Nothing*

Personal.

*But I'm tired; tired of Playing Games and shit-fuck **EXHAUSTED** of keeping Secret Friends and Lovers. Shit takes up too much time: High-Maintenance Drama. Fuck, I avoid High-Upkeep **Bitches** like the plague!!*

*No matter how I look at this shit, I reach the same Conclusion: I gotta get outta this place; the City and the Locals, their Mentalities and Ways are incompatible with me. I won't be One Dick of Many. Can't stand fake smiles and despise False Friends. I can't stand thinking she Used me and will use her Kid to hook me in again; can't **deny** it as a Strategy, since I've been-there-run-that once before. Can't think about how she never opened up to me; can't shake the Feeling of being her Dirty Little Secret... even as **FRIENDS!!!!***

Worse... can't Show these Feelings. Ever; gotta keep them bottled up. Got to Look Cool and Single when the only thing in my Heart is emptiness, pain and humiliating suffering beyond Hell. Why? Because I'm living the Lie:

don't Love you and don't give a shit about a
***damn** thing: Grinding to get the fuck outta*
Dodge.

Doesn't help that I'm Working; I Sense
everyone around me and Notice their
Movements. Adding her into the mix only
causes me to Fixate on her... everything about
her. I can smell her over the grease that needs
to be changed tonight. I Know where she is by
*the sounds she makes. Even her **breathing***
tickles Memories I just don't need; they Serve
no Purpose now and only torment my Soul
once I'm outside The Kitchen. This is what
wearing your Heart on your Sleeve will get your
*sorry ass: **HURT.***

So I replace Emotional Human Being with
O.G.; I look for the closest Female and greet
her with Big Easy Street Casual. I focus on
Servers and Cooks, watching the interplay as
Kitchen Flow follows the natural course
dictated. Got more than enough weed at the
Flop, but I check my memory to see if the
known Dealers are still around.

And... I Smell The Streets; marijuana,
alcohol, and that slow, grinding Earthy-oil

*stench, slightly Human in nature. The place Feels different as I ignore Amy and her Child; less comfortable, Happy Lie or Kitchen with Dysfunctional Family, more sickening Reality. I shoot-shit as one of the Dish Crew swaggers by, spittin' **mad** game at the new Hostess. She ain't Feelin' him and it shows; most think she's gay. Regina, lesbian and married, thinks she's too Young to know **what** she wants: Bisexual and Confused, she chuckles softly. I'd agree for now.*

"Hey, Desmond? Can I ask you for a **big** Favor?"

"Shoot, chica." My gaze slowly swings to the Speaker; this I find interesting.

"Can I drop by your place tonight? I'd like to get your opinion about something *outside* of this place." I blink; her features are Honest and Open.

"Uh... sure." *Not the Whole Story.* She smiles, offers her thanks, and bounces off, *satisfied* with herself.

"Careful, Dez." one of the other Cooks whispers. "I hear that one is psycho." I shrug, examining her Black-No.1 close-crop Hair-Do.

Not the Whole Story, **again.**

She lurks; this Thought is Important.

"Mind if I ask why, Keshan?" I ask later, when **no one** is within earshot. She bit her lip. *Fuck... something BIG is about to Go Down.*

"Well... I Seek Solace." *She expects me to Rage; too high. Thinking... and I cannot See Why she would Ask; she Lurks on my site, obviously; Vanilla Kink: Experiment with the Dark Side of Sex. Nope; not Feelin' it.*

"Huh..." I tilt my head to one side: inquisitive dog perplexed by something. She shifts her weight from foot to foot, uneasy beneath my gaze.

"Desmond. You are a Nice Guy. I wanna know why you don't bring that into this place more often."

Honest. Truth. **Foolish... but she is Willing to Take a Chance**; *she really **does** want to Understand. And it is **OH SO REFRESHING TO NOT SEE OR SENSE FEAR WITHIN A WOMAN'S EYES... AND THUS... HER SOUL!!!***

*Anger? Shit; Amy probably rounded the corner. Verified: Keshan bursts into Oh-There's-A-Baby Smile. At least it is Honest; bit unnerving that it matches the Honesty from before in Intensity. Hope she isn't a Nester... **really.** Don't know shit about her, unless you count She's-Fucked-So-and-So Gossip as Truth; can be confirmed.*

"How about Break Bread with me." She lurks, so... Besides *Amy Broke my Heart.*

"Ok..." I hear doubt creep into her tone, though it is only after Noticing Amy's Mask crack slightly; she **still** doesn't like seeing me with another Female.

* * * *

I catch Keshan off guard; she expected to be ushered into my bedroom. Instead I politely ask Keshan to sit on the sofa, playing Perfect Genteel Southern Host for the moment. You'd have to excuse the weed-and-incense stench to complete the Image, though, or be Born-and-Raised in any Home in Da Hood.

"Sorry; issues for the Moment." I dart my gaze to my smart phone, grim satisfaction rippling across my eyes as I catch the brief green LED flash from the power/status indicator.

"Well... I wanted to get naked." Keshan flashes her best Smile. My Response: I blink.

"Well?" I make my way to my bedroom, tucking my smart phone into one pocket as she rises, removing her blouse; part of me wants to look at her golden body, but I **need** a **BIG** hit from Terrorcore, my glass bong. I excuse myself, waving at her to continue, tossing in a passable Plays Devil-May-Care/Appreciative-of-the-Female-Form Smile/Grin before steppin' into my room. After two massive inhales and both lungs coughed up, I return, closing my bedroom door before swinging my legs back into the living room. She's naked by now, and I'm slightly disappointed: no hose on those svelte gams. I study her like an Artist studies a Nude Model, only I stripped Erotic from the Image Description. She ain't ugly or anything, **far** from it. I do not require those Emotions for my Question:

"Why?"

"You are more than the Kitchen; everyone knows it. No one knows you **outside** of the Kitchen except Chef and he won't tell anyone." Keshan sits with Perfect Posture; most *people cannot Relax when birth-ass naked before a complete stranger.*

"Why Naked?" I mentally check the temperature: her nipples are rock hard.

"**SEX?!?!?**" She sighs, her first relaxed movement. "Look, I know you know I Read; I'm **not** stupid."

"Never said you were; just the Opposite."

"Thank you!" She smiles; it is appealing, but Dazzles a bit too much. "No one knows what you're like in bed. I wanna be the first."

"And you'll run back and tell them everything, *starting* with how you stripped?"

"Yes." She pauses.

Here it comes; she wants Trust; no clue How to Ask for it, so she took her cue from my Tales: Solace.

"Fine. We'll start with Cleansing your Body; I like to Eat off of Clean Plates, don't you?"

"Depends; I like Sucking Dick. **Just not TOO Man-funkish!!!**"

Now I sputter-laugh; rare is the Black Female who **admits** to enjoying giving Head; refreshing that she lowers her Guard a bit. Server Keshan slowly fades from view as Keshan-the-Social Creature eases into her flesh. Her nipples respond, shrinking visibly as I make my way towards the front door.

"Until I say *Manners* you may Speak Freely and ask me anything. As for Limits..."

"What is a Plaything to you? I came across the term in another story from someone else." I stop my hand from reaching for the lock, turn and begin Explaining.

"To some, the submissive has no Free Will. There are variations on this, though." I look into her eyes, though there isn't one iota of Lust within my gaze. Instructing is something Natural for me.

"Do you have a variation?"

I face her fully. Keshan rises, confident that whatever scheme had worked. I take one step, my left hand filled with moist, wet pussy.

"Need a shave?"

"I use cream." Her voice breaks. I feel her crotch grow warmer.

"Low Boiling Point?" I chuckle. She nods; when she speaks I Hear very little Control.

"That... and I'm **dying** to know what you're like. And..." *FEAR. Gonna drop into Depression again.* "And I like Rough Sex; not sure about clothespins on the breasts, but they are sensitive." She whimpers as I grind my palm into her turgid clit, batting her eyes as she tries to maintain her stance. Her fingers flex, telling me how long she's Lurked *and* which Story Elements are running through her Mind.

"You won't get Love, just Passion." *Sadness, but...; it ain't me.* "He broke your heart more than you've let anyone know. I'm sorry."

Every Wall crumbled. She **was** Horny; she wanted Sex... Dick... however you choose the Phrasing. Yet now all she *craved* was to be Held by Loving Arms; just like that... Sex Moment Shattered.

"Yeah... and...; you won't believe me... but I wanted to talk to you about it. Strange... but... I've always looked up to you for some reason. Maybe it's the Father Figure thing... only you LOOK..." Her eyes met mine; she fell silent.

"I grant you Solace within these Walls,

Keshan. Learn well and quickly. I have Needs that must be Attended to this evening." She nods; I pinch her clit. **HARD.**

"*Manners.*"

The Hiss; foolish Child; don't rouse the Beast from its slumber.

"Yes, Sir; sorry Sir."

* * * *

Wrong; her Tone is Wrong.

Fascinating that she **hears** this as well, stammering to correct **it**, not the Words. She isn't adjusting her Tone for **submissive**; this is Street. She is in the presence of an older, wiser (she hopes... and Fears) Black **Man.** If I were to glance up, I would not be surprised to see Church pews and the old woman sitting where the Deaconesses sit, eyes fixed in

Judgmental Elderly, ghosting into being, the pulpit lit by stained-glass murals as Pastor rips out another Sermon, and I Know there is a Bible resting on the podium, one slender gold book mark placed carefully in the seam. Keshan even moves her arms, *suddenly* ashamed of being naked and crudely inspected, and her Stance lacks the Street Taught confidence from earlier.

"First Lesson   I am a Cuddle-Whore. If you have issues touching **any** part of my body, get dressed now and leave. Second: Follow Instructions, and the First Instruction: **Relax and enjoy yourself.** This ain't Slavery; you have Free Will."

"There are just... Limits."

There is something... fulfilling... about watching Understanding spark within someone. She smiles slowly, and from Church Raised, comes Seasoned, Sexually-Active Female. Were she raised in Da Hood Proper I'd call it Player Checkin' the Rules.

"Be gentle with my butthole. And... No permanent marks; purple on the ass if it feels good."

If?

I smile.

VERY slowly.

MIXED MESSAGE

Talk of Work is inevitable; I don't dance around Topics, neither does Keshan. At least I have the Excuse of being Stoned. A Stoned Babbler, she let fly with more than she expected, and is surprised to find herself less stressed. And I don't pump her for information; it comes freely and without a steep Price. All she wants to know is Why I avoid Black Females.

It's not that I avoid them. The stereotypical Black Female simply doesn't find me attractive. I don't dress *ahead* of the Fashion Sense, blazing trails; my Style comes from the Sprawl.

"Take the Hooded Scowl; plenty of Thugs with it and now they sport Rosaries."

"Tell me about that. You were wearing it *years* before anyone here, and a few people joked about it." She let one hand fade over the hematite rosary, the mineral leeching warmth from her as well as my bare chest.

"I know," I sighed, remembering one Mother who had it out with her teenaged son when she spotted him with one, *though not ONE WORD about the Gang Colors he flew!!!* "This is my Observation: Black Males are taught to Grind, Hustle, Work Hard, Play Hard. Guilt? Nope; just lay everything down at Jesus' Feet. Hypocrisy, since most Blacks scoff at the Catholic Idea of Confession and Guilt. The real Issue is this: we don't like the Idea of a Get Outta Jail Free Card. **Judgment we're familiar and comfortable with**; I wear my Rosary to Remember: I should feel Guilty for the Shit I do just to see another Day. But try as I might, can't See it in my Soul."

Strange topic to be discussing with a tit in my Hand? Maybe to someone else. She remains quiet, staring at my face for a few moments before burying her head in my chest. I caress her flesh idly, smiling as a Happy Memory filters through my post-Sex hazed Thoughts: she's just gotten her Hair-Do (my mother did hair; Good Memories from Way Back).

"You're..." A smile creeps onto her lips as she marvels at the expression, so uncommon on my Face while working.

"Careful," I chuckle. Keshan grins.

"I gotta go pee. Why does watching a Woman pee turn you on so much?"

"Let's go." She stiffens. My Reply was casual, *dismissive* actually.

"That; you don't like being watched there; few do. We're vulnerable then, Humans, and in general don't like anything disturbing us while we Think Deep Thoughts; since this is often the case when we're in the bathroom."

"Do you like people being afraid of you?"

"No. Fear, the Emotion, is Food to this...
part of me."

She sits on the toilet. I go silent, riding my
High by thinking about some music until I can
Hear the Bass Line; it takes her a few moments
to accept my Presence. I wait until the stream
tinkles against the porcelain before making a
sound, one overly noisy inhalation of Air, and
even then it startles her.

"What got you started cooking?" She
blinks, stunned by her Question apparently.
She spits a brief chuckle, covering her mound
until she notices the disapproving scowl
suddenly on my Features.

"Huh... got bored with engineering while at
college. I like learning, but *that* information was
slow coming. I was working as a cook to help
finance my School and pathetic Social Life
when it just happened. School became the
time wasted while I waited for the Weekend and
Work in the Kitchen. Hard damn Work, and as
pissy as Customers get... every now and again
I make a Happy Memory, a Moment of Peace...

sometimes I'm the Ghost Unseen when a couple remembers that romantic dinner. Now... your turn: what do you **think** I'll do to you? Here. Now."

"Actually, I want to see your dick. You're still clothed."

Yep, still wearing Social Gear: two pair of jogging pants, though the black fedora is on the coffee tale in the Living Room... Social Error.

"Thanks, gotta put my fedora up." I step from the bathroom, chuckling as I babble the Words my grandfather told me, back when I was just young enough to Remember his gaunt face.

"What?!?!"

"Social Error: no Hats on Tables."

"You're strange."

I grin broadly, flicking a cock-sure smirk to her as I tilt my head slightly.

"Oh... you're just *now* figuring this shit out?" She laughs; I like the Sound.

See... there's no Black Bitch, just a **HUMAN** Tone, devoid of Social Barriers and stigma, preconceptions and, most importantly, **DECEIT!!!**

"You wanna wipe me?"

"Nope; finish up. But before you do, ask yourself a few Questions. You do this many times: Piss, Wipe... and on a few of those occasions, at least I hope, plop that **same** urine-stained pussy onto a mouth. Is it Nasty? Freakish? **OR JUST A PART OF LIFE WE CAN'T AVOID???** Clean is a Lie, a *comfortable* Lie, but still a Lie; there is no way to get around Sex being Nasty; we sweat after all. This is *part* of the **PROCESS:** Dirty...

Clean... Dirty again; 'round and 'round, so long as we keep breathing. I Understand this, and it doesn't offend me; got my Red Wings: eating menstruating vagina." She makes a face. "See? Doesn't set well with you, and I'll bet you have your Cycle turned into Instinct to avoid it. Only Natural that you don't find a guy who **likes** that attractive... but how in the hell can you accurately tell that just by looking at his *shoes?!?!?*"

"True dat," she sighs, flushing the toilet.

Her ass is near my Right Hand. I place it on one cheek; she stops. Not rigid, just expectant. I raise one eyebrow, leaving it there just long enough for her to see as she turns her head.

"Don't take this the Wrong Way... Sir; you're the kind a Girl Marries."

I spit the chuckle as pure rancid Evil threatens to seize control of my Hands and choke Life from her lungs. "Yeah... heard that

way too many times; I'm not Disposable Dick. I don't treat Females like that, and I've fucked a few strippers. Never Disposable; always treated them as Human Beings. Guess that's why they always looked at me as if they were shellin' out a Pity Fuck: Good Guy just needs to get Laid."

"If you **only** knew; I think *everyone* believes you need some Pussy, Desmond. I mean..." Her BODY shifts. My Hand shoots the Reality before my eyes, and my eyes narrow dangerously. I raise my hand, the smile and softly snorted chuckle easing her concern while stopping the Street Taught Fuck-Ready-Seductress I see beginning to crawl into her.

"Probably true, but I don't Ho Hop. This is a Hook-Up, with a few Twists to the Rules."

"Oh, really? So... if I *really* want to suck your dick right now..."

"Does it **burn** within you?"

An Urban Gothic Romance

She moves her gaze to my semi-stiff dick; I watch her face, and bear Witness to the Social Creature Mask's evaporation; she's got an Oral Fixation. Jokes about it... but if she lets her Guard down, like now... **and** you take time to Know her... *she fights a very common Inner Battle: is she a Slut, Whore, or some other derogatory Term?*

* * * *

Sex is enjoyable: Truth. Pleasure and Morals will always be at odds where Sex is concerned: Fact.

Passion is the Essence of this War, an eternal battle everyone faces, even those who abstain. So, it helps to Understand Passion as a Process. Thought of like this, the Question Arises: Where does the Human begin and that primal thing end? The Answer is, to many, terrifying: **wherever and whenever you see fit**. The notion of dropping ones Humanity and picking it back up is somehow unnerving.

To me, it is as simple as picking up my fedora and picking off a piece of lint, brushing off real or imagined dirt. Keshan **wants** to reach this level of Maturity, for want of better Terminology. Gonna take Time and Experience... good, bad and all points between, betwixt and all around. But she has a head start.

"I don't want the guy to **only** look at me that way, ya know?"

"How many of the Servers only know me as That Mean Ol' Voodoo Nigga, hun? Trust me: I Understand Judgmental Target Fixation from others."

"Yeah.." she snuggles into my arms. "Is this... smart?"

"What? Afterglow Cuddling? Probably not, but consider this: you're here to **get** that Comfort. Wise... Smart: they enter the picture after Heartbreak and sadness, **usually**. You thought long and hard about this and *still* ended up facing that Crossroads. Keep Livin' hun.

You ain't alone in Needing this to the point
where you'll curl up at night, tears flowing;
Solitude is pure Hell if you have any Feelings at
all. Enjoy the Moment... **all** of them; and stop
Thinking: tends to ruin the Mood." I chuckle,
stroking her hair casually. She purrs as she
snuggles into my chest, her hands toying with
the nappy tangle on my chest.

"Can we try the clothespins now?"

"Why?"

"Is it strange to say I know **that** it will hurt,
but *you won't Hurt me?*"

"Thank you for the Trust, and no it is not
Strange... to me that is."

Amy said the exact same thing.

* * * *

"You work tomorrow?"

"Nope; off unless Chef needs me. Otherwise, **VACATION!!!** You?"

"LUCKY!! Nope; may I take a hit in parting? I'm a light-weight."

"Sure. C'mon."

She follows me into my bedroom; she looks around, but doesn't immediate cross the threshold.

"Kinda looks like I expected." She smiles, shaking her head as memories of *her* contribution to the Chaos slide behind her eyes.

"How **should** a bachelor's room look, if **not** like Organized Chaos? I **am** a Bachelor!"

"I mean afterwards: you'd never know anything happened here."

"Unless you knew where to Look; the Seal of Solace, Keshan:"

"Trust me, Desmond: I'll never tell a Soul that you're just a Good Man with a kinky side."

TO DINE WITH DEMONS

Every now and again a Cook has to do a
Meet and Greet; means smiling, laughing and
in general, behaving like you actually **have** a
shred of Humanity within you. Of course, once
you get back Behind the Scenes you can safely
drop the Mask. I never like Meet and Greets.
To me it means putting on The Political Face,
standing with cool confidence born from smiling
often and using gracious, sweet Lies for Words
and gestures. So when one of the Servers
loudly proclaims that I have a visitor, someone
who asked for me, it takes a few moments to
wiggle into that uncomfortable Skin. The Mask
doesn't feel right, like dust and slime coat its
inner surface. I take several breaths, refocus
my Mind and Thoughts. Then I take several
more, as infinite Darkness is difficult to escape
or completely conceal. Doesn't help that my
visitor is Female. Everyone there suddenly
becomes interested in me. Two seconds
before the Proclamation, everyone there either
despised my existence or loathed it, Fear

pounding behind every heartbeat: another crappy Shift on the Line.

Imagine my surprise when stepping into the Dining Area. My gaze snaps immediately to the long, dusty blonde hair. I Register the Customers, file away the Details and smile as the Lies fade away. I forget my surroundings and the stares from Servers and Management alike as *laughter* rumbles from my chest. Honest, Joyous Laughter of the kind that feeds and maintains Happiness **feels** wondrous. For once, God Hears Praise and Thanks from my Soul, and for the Moment, Darkness pulls back. Its Movements stem from Respect, and its exodus lays bare a whimpering Fear. It scurries back, desperate in its search for the cruel Warmth that Darkness torments it with. And when she rushes into my arms...Everything stops. I bask in the Moment, thankful for it. It is Good, and beyond Word-restraint/confinement.

It's coming...

"Hoi, Demon,' she purrs softly. She slides her hands from my chest, draping them around

my neck as my arms *gratefully* encircle her
Body, laughter dabbling about her lips as my
scruff refuses to release a few of her locks.

"How fare you this 'eve, Maiden Most
Fair?"

And for once, I let everyone See...
something Different.

* * * *

"Gonna introduce us?"

For the Love of all that is
UNHOLY!!!!!!!!!!!!!!!!!!!!!!

Gone... just like that. I recognize the Voice
and Vow to make their SOUL suffer for daring
to intrude on this Moment. I turn with measured
pace, holding her in my right arm as Images of
hideous, razor sharp demon wings/sorcerous
blades slice the offender into perfect eight-inch

slices. I shield Maiden more for the Server's protection, sadly. It means she gets to see this side of me, something I hoped she'd never have to See or Experience. She wraps her arms around me, stepping into my embrace, yet she does not stop what is about to happen. Indeed, her gaze sweeps across my chest, and I Sense her own sadness at the Loss of the Moment. And then, Amy steps into view; from Unholy to insanely Demonic, my eyes brighten with savageness as I Remember.

"Ever have someone in your Life who, if they asked you to Kill someone, you would? No Questions... no Regrets?"

*"**NO!!!!!!** Do you?"*

"Yes."

Human cruelty settles over my features, a Look everyone is all too familiar with. Maiden need only point to someone... **anyone**... and I'd end their pathetic existence then and there, crushing, destroying everything and anyone

foolish enough to stand in my way. I inhale...
exhale... second breath, and that black Evil
deep within my Soul stirs. I see flashes from its
Nightmarish Wet-Dreams, frightened faces
illuminating oblivion's depths faintly. Innocent...
Innocence... Guilt... *playthings*. It smells Fear
rise from Human Flesh. Fear... sweet nectar;
and I see Amy swallow.

"Demon." Maiden scratches the nape of
my neck. My eyes lower as Reality cowers its
way back into being.

Even so, Fear's unholy Strength now flows
through my veins, pulses through heartbeats. I
don't breathe so much as growl, low... ominous.
I hear glasses clink nervously. There are a few
Thugs here; I smell gun-oil, coke and good
weed smoke heavy over the dirt shit they hawk.
Reality; some of the Servers find someplace
else to focus their attention; Management
adjusts its Professional Mask, devoid of that
insidious Fake Friend. One can't help it; I
ignore the slight: can't fight Genetics.

They aren't Human. I smile, letting pure
Evil explode across my eyes as it morphs into
Politically Correct for a ruthless sack-of-shit;

now I Look like them.

Amy watched the entire Process. If it wasn't for someone asking her about her Child, I'm unsure how she would have Recovered. As it stood, the interruption gave me just enough Time to slide Maiden into a quiet corner and *politely* beg off from any further introductions... or incidents.

* * * *

"Jo-Jo? You gonna make a play for Dez's friend?"

"Fuck no; he'd kill me and anyone who got in the way. Didn't you see that look on his face when Amanda opened her mouth?" Yeah. Always wondered where Desmond got the nick-name Demon.

His friend looks like... well; I've imagined her in a flowing Victorian Robe. And yeah, those firm tits are a big part of why I think that,

45

but the **way** they interacted makes more than one call him Bougie. I know better because I always thought Desmond was a Good Guy: capital letters there.

And Desmond is her Body Guard, one *literally* from Hell. There are times when he stands there, wringing his neck. Looks like something is trying to claw its way out, and he's struggling to keep it in. And by struggle, I don't mean he's afraid of it; he **wants the Power that damned things has for his OWN truly sick ends!!!** Something about Desmond always strikes me as unfulfilled Mass Murderer. Serial Killing took too much Planning, and while Dez plans everything, not Killing. Maybe it is the outright insanity he occasionally shows when he twists his face up Joker-from-Batman like.

And this Woman holds the reins. One look from her and the offending fucker tryin' to Spit Game will find their throat exposed to air, watching as their blood gushes into the atmosphere. And she looks like the type who knows, **just KNOWS**, that somewhere there is a situation that Requires Demon's unique Skills and Abilities. **That** Thought chills me, probably more than watching Desmond slowly return to Human-Self as he introduces her to everyone.

Everyone except Amy; she slid to the bathroom. I know why.

But to see that evil thing flash across Desmond as he watched/not-watched her flee (and make no mistake, **Amy Ran**), I wonder what *exactly* went down between them. And just like that I feel something punch through my Grave and choke the Ghost inside the casket; blink, and Desmond is looking **directly** at me.

Shit!!!!!!! I swallow. When he gets like this...

"Hey McScruff, can I see your Kitchen?"

"Sure hun, if Management allows it, that is."

We speak politely as one of the Managers chimes in, eager to show off the new Broil. Just happens to be Desmond's Home, and for some reason, that just seems right. I shake off the roller coaster Emotions and go back to Serving. Like some of the others, seeing that... *thing...* crawl over him is...

I need a set of Tits to look at; over there...

Happy Thoughts... Happy Thoughts...

* * * *

"You think Desmond and..."

"Don't; sayin' his name is Bad Ju-Ju."

"Bullshit... and I'll bet *she* knows how he got the name Demon!! Just because he knows Voodoo doesn't mean he's some Big Bad!!"

"Uh-huh... sure." Amanda doesn't believe it one bit. No one there does. "Think about him and all sorts of dark thoughts enter your head;

I've read some of his stories; some... make me nervous. He ain't stable, not by a long-shot."

"She picked him up after work; did you see how he ran outta here!!"

More bullshit; they are not gonna like it when their Dreams turn into freakish Nightmares tonight. Better drink until you can't remember them; that's My Plan tonight.

* * * *

She's never seen me High; before bouncin' I found a Circle and joined in. The Dish Crew joked with me a bit, but they avoided outright askin' if we were gonna fuck. Respect; they Know Who she is.

Let me explain: she's beyond Family... above Blood. They won't Fuck with that Image. Street Law says Killing is **HOW** you Deal with such Disrespect. Only Fuckin' with a Man's Money comes above the Love I have for her.

So I'm somewhat apprehensive about her smelling it on me, and I actually check to see if it offends her... in our Silent Communication... which she breaks:

"Stepping Through, Sir." *Holy...*

Tonight of **all** Nights; a truly amused grin splits my lips.

"Are you sure?"

"No, but I Trust you, Demon. That... and you need it McScruff. I saw you back there. Are you OK?"

"Not by a long-shot, hun. This your Ride?"

"Solace, Old Friend." She shakes her head, and I get lost in her Presence, forgetting the crap for a blessed Moment.

The Maiden and The Demon

An Urban Gothic Romance

"Zoom; and get ready to be crushed by some heavy shit. I won't hold back."

"Neither will I " Something about that...

"Maiden?" She lowers her head slowly. I See the Words on her Features; they tear at my Heart. I Know what will come from her lips; I've fantasized about them. I place my fingers over her lips. "Are you Sure?"

She shakes her head, eyes wide; can't help but nearly choke on her Scent. Arousal of the Female Form is Known, but **this** Passion runs deep; as Deep as I feared when I first lay eyes upon her beautiful face, forever Dazzled.

"No going back."

"And you won't leave me."

There you have it then; I sit back in the passenger seat, terrified as we creep through the night. I take long, calming pulls from my one-hitter Grim, though the weed does nothing to soothe the fascinating Reality I approach as familiar Night Scenes drift by. I even forget the awesome power of the hurricane, and something within me desperately cries out, demanding its Say: Memories of Katrina. I long to cry on her shoulders, for Everything to come spilling out; mangled Thoughts and Emotions.

Sex? If you want to piss me off, mention it; it **will** Happen, but it isn't Necessary. Inevitable and considered pitiful, it won't truly Express our Feelings and can easily fuck up a Life-Long Friendship. **What-If?** Coulda... woulda... shoulda. We're gonna fuck this up, and don't really care. We'll both be there, helping each other pick up the Pieces, just as we've always done. Together.

Can't stop imagining her Thoughts as she shifts gears. Can't stop the lustful Thoughts, and give up on Dark Thoughts completely as we pull into the Gas-and-Go. I slip in, grab a **pack** of cigarillos. Street Sense catches her outside of her car, arms folded up, before I actually see her. I smile... a Pimp's cock-sure grin easing into my Soul as I Notice her stance. Bold; the Strength of her Soul outshines the lone light overhead right before everything fades into a strangely quiet dark as I pull her close. Her Scent obliterates the Street Funk.

"Regrets... later."

"Agreed."

SOLACE WITHIN

By the time the car's engine is dead-and-silent, every Shadow in My Hood: visually violated: nothing Moves that I don't Notice; if she didn't touch my left arm *tenderly*, I would exit the rental in pure Street Warrior Mode: Ready for Death. I **still** do, though it isn't Soul consuming.

We grab her things, and I'm actually caught off guard by how ***STREET*** her Movements are. She doesn't look at me, keeping her eyes squarely focused on her actions while subtly swinging her head this way and that, picking up the new Sounds greeting her ears. Yet I am **always** within her line of sight. I grab the two biggest suitcases, ignoring Thoughts of their contents as I felt my eyes narrow: *she looks like Money.*

I don't have any Deep Thoughts as I unlock the door. I swing my gaze over her head as she ducks inside, checking for any movement. I hear Ghost Dancer's paws crunch the soft, drying grass as he comes for his Nightly Snack. Getting it means going inside, returning to the Night, then back inside: **plenty** of Time to Think Shit Through.

"Ghost Dancer's outside." Maiden smiles, standing patiently in the middle of her things. I eye this arrangement, raising one eyebrow mirthfully as I jet to the fridge for a slice of turkey, Dancer's favorite snack.

And though it only takes a few Moments, my MIND fills with Thoughts. I wasn't expecting Company during my Vacation, **certainly** didn't expect this. We'd *talked* about spending time together, Playing Catch Up. **THIS...** will go far beyond pleasant conversation. Fresh memories of her tongue sliding over mine, the way her hands *clawed* at my clothed Flesh, exploded in my Mind as I dove back into the white-light Night shadows. Dancer stretched his head, peering into the place before chowing-down on the sliver of meat in his food dish.

Yes, old Friend: There awaits Change and Chaos. Time to Face... a Mistake yet Made.

Inside, I close the door, making little Show about securing the locks. I look at Maiden. She stands there, beautiful beyond description. What I **must** do next doesn't bother me: *that SHE is there... that she WANTS, maybe* **NEEDS** *to be Here... Now...* **with me...**

There is nothing Gained in hesitation.

"Strip." It wasn't a full-blown Command; my Tone was akin to Friendly Doctor, minus anything Clinical. I wanted to see if she would hesitate; she did.

When she begins removing her clothes I watch Fear ripple through her. Fantasy is one thing, now we were going to shatter a shared Rule: No Sex Between Friends. Why? August 29, the anniversary of Hurricane Katrina. It will be six years, and this is the first time I will have someone to hold when everything comes rushing back.

She's afraid I'll frown up, disappointed by her body; I'm *actually* doing everything possible to keep calm as I Feel Memories from Those Waters suddenly clamor for attention, now that The Outside World was Sealed Off. A curious form of Absolution, our impending Sex, and I consider it such **because** she is apprehensive. She will soon see me at my utter most vulnerable, simpering with terror as Images flash across my mind. Once she is naked, she tries to cover up her privates.

"Back during Katrina, I heard plenty of Sex went down, and I don't mean the rapes. People were still Bumpin' Uglies, probably driven by terror and the Need for comfort. Don't know. All I Know is that place was a cesspool, and **still...** Primal urges."

She holds out her arms, slowly; I look into her eyes as my easy smile slips into Memory. I remain motionless, overcome with those haunting Memories. I don't immediately register her until something pulls me back from those Waters, black-brackish, coated with oil, gasoline and only God knows what else. *A*

*lone child, crying on cardboard covered with
sand, piss and the detritus from Humanity's
near-Collapse... A Failure I can Share **ONLY**
with her, yet do not.* I turn, forcing my eyes to
see her face; yet it isn't until I smell her tears
do I return to Reality, torn from Images of the
Superdome now too-vivid within my Mind's Eye.

Funny; dropping my emotional baggage on
her wasn't part of the Plan. Yet she **is** here for
me: Good, Bad, Bruised and Ugly. I caress
her bare back. Lust is there, but it **waits
RESPECTFULLY** as my Thoughts settle, the
Smell of Sprawl and Human Desperation
blowing away gently, carried by her Scent...
and her Tears.

"My Sadness can wait, My Dear." She
sobs quietly, snuggling into my arms. I feel Life
slowly pour into my arms. Energy flows
through leg muscles, and as I take in Fresh Air,
my High (*I'd completely forgotten I'd toked up;
couldn't feel its effects while Remembering*)...

"Happy Thought?"

She chuckled... right before poking me; I squeaked.

* * * *

This may be cynical, but I'm done Remembering that Nightmare. All I want is to Move Forward. There are a few things I must accomplish, and I'm neck-deep In the Weeds. Sitting on the sofa, still dressed for the Streets, I stroke her hair and Think about what I am going to do next; her Sacrifice might be in vain, and even though I knew there would be Pain, she was Right: I will never leave her side; we'll get through together.

"Think I need a hit, hun." She moans, then rises. I lead her into my bedroom, the Chamber of Sorrows as we call it.

"It looks like you," she chuckles.

"What? Utter shitpile?"

"**NO!!!** Organized Chaos!!" I get goosed for being a smart ass.

I undress without fanfare or Strip Tease.

"Does yours have a Name?"

"Bad Bad Leroy Brown; baddest Dick in the whole damn Town!" I flash my cock-sure grin, shaking my semi-erect member as I reach for a pair of jogging pants.

"You're getting dressed?"

"And *your* laptop is in the living room; time for Social Management; wanna see who is Reading and check a few things."

"I'll get it later. Right now, I wanna watch you Think." She smiles, sitting cross-legged on my bed. I chuckle, reach for my bowl and a lighter.

"Pardon the smoke."

"May I?"

"Sure, if you tell me why?"

"Already did," she puckered her lips, the motion making her entire body *shine!!*

I don't laugh when she coughs/chokes.

"Thank you for Breakin' Bread with me, Maiden."

"Thank you for not being disgusted with my Body McScruff."

"FIE!! I **like** what I see."

Careful. She Smiled; *too late.*

* * * *

I suck at flirting, but give me a good buzz, fantastic company and Opportunity, I make due. Never gave being high much thought before Sex. Did so with her because it notched one of her Personal Fantasies: Sex while High. She survived college, so **drunk** Sex is thrice-notched and secure... same here. And the Sex, while Great, became the Time Between Snuggle Sessions. During our current Session she asked me something peculiar:

"You haven't had sex in your chair; why not?"

"Business gets done in that Seat My Dear; Sex is pure Pleasure... and for the record, being blown while I'm in this chair **is** Biz: Need a Nut, not Emotions."

"Huh?"

"Here; sit. Now... Feel the Moment." She sighed, a chuckle slipping from her several seconds later. *Hey: Naked Ass on the Chair!!!*

"Damn; you're **right!!!**" I shrugged, flipping her legs over the arm rests, much to her delighted surprise.

The soft ping of a Facebook Chat popped in a full two seconds after her orgasm. I swallowed her nectar, mentally tearing the Soul from the fucker who dared bother me while I Feasted. Clearing the screen saver I let my gaze wander to the chat request, and when it landed on the name, I couldn't help my chuckle.

"Who is it?"

"Someone from Work who **never** chats; curious." *As-If: Nosey fuckhead wondering Why I Ghost with Pussy In-House. I hate Stupid.*

"They wonder if you're online," she sighs, planting feathery kisses on my hips.

"And ignoring you. Wonder what I should say."

I fire off a quick greeting, saying that I had company; truth, and it will keep them hovering online, watching the Time Stamp on my replies... a **long** wait.

"No music?"

"Hun, all I've got is Street Vibes and Hardcore." She shrugs, reaching for the glass bowl.

"That was..." She stared at the black-green mass.

"Stimulates Pleasure Nerves," I say, a slow smirk dangerously close to worming into my

Thoughts.

"Does that include spankings?"

* * * *

I've spanked a Girlfriend, my Ol' Lady, *several* Skripper-hoes and Random Females; Maiden makes the first Friend-you'd-Die-For, and despite the **FAINT** hesitation wringing itself into Panic deep in my gut, I find myself absolutely **NO Different Mentally.** Even the impish light dancing behind her eyes is Status Quo.

* * * *

First Position

We put her things in the Guest Room; she insists on wearing clothes for her first Spanking, though I know it won't last long. So... Why am I

on edge? Shrugging off the sensation I reload
my bowl, take two hits and begin typing; the
Words Flow with awesome Power. Then I
Sense her; the door is closed partially, and the
knock drags an unexpected emotion from me:
Annoyance.

"Enter." Flat, yet Questioning. The door
swings open. She has long hair; the Hair Do is
Classic: *thrown up in a bun, kept in place with
two hair sticks!!!* The white blouse is tucked
professionally into the waistband of the black,
form fitting *without* being **slimming** skirt. I dart
my gaze towards her feet, confirming the
overall Look, nodding, then fixing my gaze upon
My Maiden.

"May I Assist you, Sir?"

Yes we've Had Sex; yes I've tasted her
nectar as she sat in the chair I now physically
occupy. At the Moment, however, **Demon sits
on the Throne of Bones.** The Memory of that
Conversation **appears**, yet it does not linger. I
Feel hideous, Ancient Thoughts seize still-
frames from my Memory, tossing aside the
ones that do not Fit Here/Now. I Remember
how her vulva felt beneath my lips, yet the mere

THOUGHT of them shielded by Hose...
**Covered by Humanity's Need to be Seen as
Normal...** *This is How she appears... when
we were closest to making this very Mistake;
Fitting, perhaps.*

And Strange to consider this odd Truth:
when she makes a typo and I Punish her (Five
Falls from my belt), **THIS IS WHEN WE MAKE
LOVE!!!**

This... is When the Nightmare stirs.

THIS ONE DREAM

It tears its way from the abysmal, infinite depths, howling... driven mad by Existence. Thoughts flood its frame. Demonic wings rip into being, tearing away Reality as they search for purchase upon the hideous Creation's back. It flexes powerful arms as razor sharp obsidian claws spring forth. It gazes into its palms as flashes of everything appears in its Mind. The Pain lessens, replaced by The Hunger; it will grow slowly, the Creature knows; it will Consume; there can be no other way. It breathes, foul, noxious Truth rolling from its snout/nostrils; inhale, and everything Holy cringes: it Smells Fear.

Again and again, it trembles excitedly clenching its powerful jaw muscles. Click-clack go scales as legs flex. Sweat fills its Thoughts... Sweat from Fear. Slowly it breathes in the sweetness. Long and cruel, covered in black ichor, its tongue writhes about

inside its maw, occasionally caressing one fang
or another.

MORE...

Again and again, though there is patience
within the form, wings kissed by unseen winds
flutter, the decayed-flesh holes whispering
Forbidden Hymnals. It stretches its neck, eyes
now squarely fixed on the kaleidoscopic Chaos
flowing before its Notice.

Here Fishy Fishy...

Like thunder... like the roar of Unholy Hosts
charging up a hill of broken dreams and
bones... the Creation Chuckles as it observes
its Human Prey.

And I blink, smile, and greet yet another
Day.

* * * *

She held me; why... I do not know.

"Demon?"

"Hmmm?" The utterance rides a savageness that fades, whipping angrily as my Flesh warms to her Presence.

"Have you ever had The Dream while high?"

"I don't dream at all when I'm high... or at least I don't remember them, and **that** is one damned good Reason to *stay* at least buzzed before bedtime." It fades slowly; I stretch even slower, my Movements twitching a snarl as I adjusted to my flesh.

"And you smoke before work... why?"

"I'm a Cook; you do **NOT** go into The Kitchen Sober if you Cook or Serve. Dealing with The Public takes... a *certain* Twisted Mindset from jump; calm-the-nerves/get-yer-head-in-the-game. Back in New Orleans it wasn't uncommon to have a Cook come in with Skripper Funk and Glitter all over 'em." She chuckles, rolling onto her stomach. I Notice that being watched didn't bother me.

"I remember."

That's right... Though only through emails and chat, we stayed in constant touch. She's gotten more than a few Drunk Rants; seen me blather on when Death was the only Companion I knew.

"Gonna show me Your Sprawl, Old Wolf? It **is** Daylight." The only time a **LADY** is ever seen, as I recall writing.

* * * *

By daylight the town looks like any other quietly dying Genteel semi-Sprawl in Virginia; Money follows Style and Land, so spotting such Houses all in one general area is standard issue, and something she knows very well from back home. She wasn't as familiar with the Dying Suburbs (Da Hood), however, as I've come to Know the deceptively simple Homes dotting winding roads where getting lost is **expected from LOCALS!!!**

"Stop."

"What?" My Senses go into Overdrive.

"That, Sir; stop."

"The Thug Look." **NOW** it makes sense.

"It doesn't suit you, Sir."

"Too much Big Easy?"

"Too little."

I smile softly: she's very cute when frowned up in Thought. Just cute enough to let Street Sense slip, and with a pat to one knee I nod, the chuckle soft yet full as I round a corner. *Cop Up Ahead!!* I flick my gaze towards the hill, and the corner I knew lay just ahead, partially obscured by the Donk and the Hyundai SUV, trees, Big Wheels and bushes lined up on one side and the crumbling concrete wall failing to impede the red dirt Front yard of the condemned flop across the street: Our Side of the road.

Officer Bad Ass rolls over the corner at Lazy Speed, politely presses his brakes once as he spots our car, then his black Ray-Bans zeroes in on Driver. My jaw twitches when I see him visibly tense up, his right hand sneaking to his computer terminal.

"Smile," she mutters.

"Then he **will** pull us; watch." My lips

barely move and I make no show of moving my eyes to meet his, but as we pass I jerk my head up slightly; his slow nod: Country Boy Proud.

"Ritual?"

"Welcome to Da Hood, m'Lady Fair."

"Any others I should know about?"

"That would be why I asked you to bring your camera; we're gonna take one picture of a local landmark."

"One frequented by police?"

"It also happens to stand at The Crossroads; from this one spot you can take one road into old Town, where the old Money Families hold absolute Power over the **entire** town. Take another and we're in a different Hood, one I **also** know from my Young Scamp Days. Huh..."

"What?"

"That's where I got my First Kiss I think, back in that Hood. Back then there was a Butcher's Market." As if on cue, **both** stomachs roar.

"Ok... change of plans?" I manage after our laughter subsides.

* * * *

"Once we're back inside..."

"Take me, Sir." I raise one eyebrow, unlock the door and let her enter first; kicking the door closed I Seize her hair, quite literally without Thought. She hisses, coming to a halt immediately. I feel her start turning towards me; I lift my Hand as I swivel around, slightly confused about the best way to Secure the Front Door with my Left Hand.

"Hold Still." She Complies.

"Better." I Release her, check the locks, **then** turn around to face her, my arms instantly folding up behind me: Morpheus Bound.

None of my Actions surprise me because of the very polite, **very** Turned-On Woman staring at me, Lust tugging a smile on her lips as she tries not to fidget.

"Sober, there are No Excuses, Sir; you Taught me that."

Indeed. My arms unfurl from my back as I make my way towards her. Without my High, Lust is not only slow to boil, there is nothing stopping my Thoughts from focusing on the hideous Void I suddenly find myself surrounded by. Sober, I Know I won't simply Go for the Pussy. Sober, I'll THINK about what I'm doing, and in the end, deep down within me, the Word *Violate* burns not-so-quietly.

"Cum for me; you have thirty Seconds, and do not touch yourself. Begin." I walk around her, moving through her Aura and Thoughts.

"I..."

"If you Fail me you will be Punished, Slut."

She failed, stammering an apology. I unbuckled her slacks from behind her, jerking them down unceremoniously, leaving her ass covered by the pink thong. I rudely cram two fingers into her anus, leaning forward as I Speak.

"You Exist to Please me, Slut. This is what you Requested. Present."

* * * *

I REALLY need to get Blitzed. It Feels as if I'm sitting in the Passenger's Seat from the moment Maiden bends over at the waist, supporting herself on the coffee table in front of her; I'm still fingering her anus, but there ain't one Thought in my head: just swirling Darkness.

"You will Follow Instructions precisely and swiftly, Slut: Reply."

"I understand, m'Lord."

"Very good; your memory is sharp. You will be Rewarded. On your knees, Slut."

No no no no no; she's Under. No denying it now. I Feel Thoughts of the Equipment flung from the Darkness, the desperate need for a Hit agonizing as I watch Maiden succumb to the submissive Slut within her.

Hold up... Replay that Memory. Sure enough: from the moment I began unbuckling my pants until the time I revealed a slowly rising member, her eyes **never** left my crotch; she worked her tongue in her mouth, betrayed by the subtle movement of her chin and the obvious swallowing. **YET...** ***never opened her Mouth!!*** Just like The Good Little Slut: a story I'd written after... after...

Do Not Look into her Eyes. I Feel my body nod and Agreement whispers in my Mental Ear as my Right hand pulls her bangs over her eyes, but not in time for me to catch her flick a Glance at me: *Thankful!!!*

She's been Here before. Sober... there are no Excuses.

Twenty lashes with the Belt; she'll cum by the tenth if I'm right. Something cold grows within me in a Place I know. Something Died here. Recently. Finish this; Gotta Think.

* * * *

Sober, there are No Excuses; so the hard cider in her hand balances the equation, since **TECHNICALLY** I am not in my Right State of

Mind... Legally. Wonder about this though:
damn near always High unless I'm off from
Work, which is **rare** these days, so by **being**
high *normally...*

Probably Liable; oh well... at least I Tried to
Lie to myself; still doesn't quite make me laugh.

"I like this."

"What? Hardcore?"

"It fits you, now that I've seen it."

"It... doesn't frighten you. Why?"

"You wouldn't look at me."

"Don't make me..."

"Don't; I won't let you. The Rule."

I snort a chuckle; contagious, we both burst into laughter. The Rule: if a Guy tells you he Loves you during sex, **especially** during orgasm, *HE'S LYING!!!!* Of course, she never looks at me while reminding me of the Rule, hiding behind taking a sip of cider while fussing with her hair: tell-tale; like me, she'd rather Speak Brutal Honesty... and using The Rule is a nice Loop Hole to exploit, especially when she doesn t believe it... at least with me. She knows better.

And if I accept, then I can always fall back on The Rule as an Excuse for any lingering Emotions. Street Law sez I can even Cock-Diesel and show my ass. Yeah... *right.* All I have to do is Have Sex with a Woman everything within me wants to Love **without** Falling in Love and...; I take another hit as my thoughts spin out of control, the action turning my back to her.

"Personal Question."

"Shoot."

"Why do you like eating pussy so much?"
Her chuckle comes with no real amusement; I
Sense her open and close her legs, verifying
with a slight turn of my head.

I turn in my chair, the slow motion
inadvertently dramatic... at least until I suddenly
realize what is happening: High doesn't just
keep me from dreaming; every now and again,
something wakes up.

"I like the taste," I mutter Honestly, trying
not to look into her eyes; this is How it starts. I
do not know if she sees the look flit across my
face. I only know what she does next:
something... **unexpected.**

"Feast."   It isn't the whisper, it is **TONE**;
forbidden Passion. I Know this Music well.

I rise slowly, scrambling to blame the
weed as she also rises. She sets the bottle on
my computer desk, the movement vivid in my
Mind. I remember... **FEAR** gripping me as I
see...

What I always see within her: a Passionate Woman. So those Moments are not pure Hollywood fluff; she *smells* fantastic, and it Howls inside my Thoughts. I feel my eyes widen, and see something flash across her lips: *a smile?!?!?*

Rush; overcome, I lose track of **everything**; then Snap-to-Reality *right* as her hair gets in the way.

I sneer.

I sneer, and I cannot claim Moment of Clarity, nor blame being High on the Thoughts white-hot in my Mind: *Man is the most savage Beast of all.*

They are Pointless: Details. Eventually, **I am Done, and let her fall to the bed Beneath Me.**

*Ease Off... Ease Off... Look elsewhere...
that's it;* **SHE IS NOT OURS... SHE IS NOT
OURS.**

* * * *

I make my way into the kitchen, wiping my
face with the cold Knowledge that the action
offered little comfort and no lasting Peace. I
Focus on the momentary Goal: quench
Biological Thirst, obliterating even the random
always-there house obstacles in my way. My
heart is racing, though I cannot feel it beating
inside my chest: too much blood rushing
through my ears; too much **LUST** powering my
Thoughts. I feel its sneer pull up my lips once,
twice, three times; each time it gets easier to
Control... me. I open the refrigerator door, the
light almost blinding me as she rounds the
corner, her hair blessedly covering her eyes. I
beat back Images both hideously seductive and
darkly beautiful.

"Water?"

"Sure."

Lame; we Need Lame right now. I can hear it trembling just beneath her breath, even as I hear that Thing **howl** inside my chest, the utterance punching through my Thoughts. I step away, giving her room while getting her a glass. I look at her, only slightly concerned by the rancid sludge-for-Thoughts worming their way into my physical reactions and movements. She'd pulled on the black robe hanging from my door: ever the Modest Lady.

Not sure which thumps louder: my Dick, or that thing where my Heart, lungs and all other internal organs used to be. I hand her the glass of water. She takes it gently by the bottom, avoiding physical contact; Nothing *Escapes Our Notice.*

"Thank you for everything." Her eyes go wide as if she let too much slip.

I turn to get my water, the movement concealing what I know my eyes betrayed: *Not Buying it.* When I face her again, a radiant smile glows behind her eyes. I lift my glass in silent toast; she answers in kind, and together we sip. One. Two. Three.

"No regrets."

"None."

"And... Cuddle?"

I smile.

I SMILE.

* * * *

Channel Surfing: Mindless Entertainment when one show simply cannot hold fascination or interest; I could always count on my Thoughts grinding to a halt once the television winked into existence. With Maiden tucked beneath my left arm, my Mind kept jumping from Brain Eradication via Media blather to the slow churn as darker Thoughts hiss-plorp-bubbled behind my features.

I flick her nose playfully before asking, "Anal... when?" She slaps my arm playfully, her chuckle sliding easily into words.

"Stop!! And don't be mad at him for this; it happened before he broke my heart. Well... it was an accident. **REALLY!!!** Only... he stopped."

"And you?"

"Oh, I stopped and didn't say a word. He pulled out slowly, babbling about being sorry. I said 'that's ok.'" *Datum.*

"The pain?"

"Hurt... like hell; and I think I came... not sure. It was *supposed* to hurt and it did."

"No one said anything about you enjoying it, though." She shakes her head sadly. I can See the memory: Emotional Waves crashing against her tender Features, *darkening* them, yet there was also Wisdom within the curious smile hovering just beneath the Sadness.

"When you put your tongue up there, everything went blank."

"Was I the first?"

She rises up and looks me in the eye, then with an odd smile splitting her lips says, "You are my First and so far only Black Lover, McScruff."

I blink before spitting out an amused chuckle. "Really?" The Blink: *does that include Females? Interesting.*

She settles back into her cuddle after the small chuckle-fit. I'd written more than one

Story about this specific encounter, yet had not yet had the dubious pleasure; the Strippers I know use Race only when it keeps them from overt Bullshit/Drama/Violence. As I held her, I mentally checked my List of Females: Maiden is the only so-called Normal MILF I've ever been with Sexually!!

"Wonder where I Fit in the Negro/Big-Dick-Nigga Legend... **OOF!!**"

"You deserved that!!" she laughed. "Besides... there's something I wanted to ask you about the White Room."

"Subject change?"

"Not really." She blushes down to her shoulders, snuggling into me as she took one steadying breath; cute.

"When you had your tongue up my ass..."

"Manners." The Word slid out, Polite yet firm in its casual utterance.

"Sorry, Sir."

* * * *

I should be concerned; I don't even bat an eye; she doesn't stop herself. Naturally submissive, she simply corrects herself and continues to explain.

"When you had your tongue up my rear, I was thinking: *that's nasty!!! Would he do that after I... went Potty?*"

"Only after Number One; I **do** have Limits, My Dear." She snuggles into me, humming/purring softly as I run my hands over her smooth skin, lazily tracing random patterns along her arms and breasts and cheeks.

"Good," she sighs comfortably, smiling into

my chest.

"Now, tell me why you didn't like being a Pimp, Sir."

"She was a Ho," I say after wrinkling my nose, gathering my Thoughts. "I don't like Hoes; they don't have Souls, hun. Female is the baseline. From there you add Mentality; Ho Mentality means your Body has a Price. Mind and Body: Sold to the Highest bidder; nothing inside the Flesh except materialistic bullshit and a Monkey on the Back. Doesn't have to be drugs; shopping is just as big on the addiction scale; habits of Humanity, I'm afraid." One corner of my lip jerks into a sneer/smirk as I Remember a few Faces, always with the Gear and Tattoos: Trappings of Individuality.

"But you didn't hit her."

"Yes, I did. She didn't have the Money from dancin': **RENT Money**. After I hit her, she **smiled** and quietly handed over the money. Acted like nothing happened, too. That's when

I Knew she was a solid Ho to the Core, and I *really* didn't want that in my flop."

"She... **liked?**"

"No; she **NEEDED** it, hun. Hard Hoes sometimes come like that: they're so used to Anger-backed Violence from Males, that they *expect* it and will not at **ALL** respect a Male who **doesn't** Treat them that way.

"I still don't get it; hope I never do."

I ponder that, and **this** concerns me.

* * * *

"Why the Change in subject, though?"

"Define Slut for me, Sir. Please." *Ah... Trying to See what I See.*

"First, only a Woman may claim to be a Slut. Women are keenly Aware of the darker, lustful Emotions churning within **HUMANITY**, not to mention their own Flesh. That it takes on... *extremes...* at times; they Deal as best they can. To me, they have a Right to Demand their Lover Understand this, or at least make Herculean efforts to do so. And when she decides to jump you... go for it; cuddle... same."

"And when she demands Pain?" *FUCK!!!* Never saw it coming; should have. Fighting down the sudden dark, lustful urges pounding in my ears isn't new; her Timing keeps me guessing.

Fascinating.

She places my right hand over her breast; it is only now that I catch her Scent, that dark, sweetly seductive Essence. I wait... And Wait.

She exhales.

"Do not anticipate." She nods, gulping.
Her gaze shifts, and Youthful Dark-Innocence
shimmers as it is replaced by something
Human in form only.

"Now do you see? Only a Woman..."
Before she can respond, I slap her breast
between my hands, the movement not
awkward, not impeded by our position: Sudden
Pain, and she, eyes wide, remains silent,
smiling with cold, cruel Lust.

* * * *

"And... afterwards... clean..."

"Indeed: Cleansing."

One Heartbeat, two bodies.

"And Hoes..."

"Either can't or Won't; which only they and God really Know. No amount of showers..."

She kisses me; I melt into it, all Thought gently vanishes on her warmth. She straddles me, adjusting slightly as I enter her.

"And... Ho Tendencies, Sir?"

A Game? How long can I continue to Focus on Teaching when Distracted?

I slide one finger up her anus; her eyes flutter, closing slightly.

"Thank me."

"Thank you, Sir," she purrs. I raise one eyebrow, smiling gently. "I see. Only a Woman, Sir." I lean down and bite one nipple; she hisses.

"Don't anticipate," I mutter around the nubbin, rolling it between my teeth. She takes my head in her hand, lifting it until I gaze into her eyes.

"And only a True Gentleman can Understand a Woman's Needs." She smiles and I Hear inside my head a satisfied exhaled breath, all too Human... all too much like Me with too much Age on me.

"And I come with a Dark Side."

"As I said... **A TRUE GENTLEMAN**, Sir"

I start to go soft inside her; her eyes... they burn: Judgment being passed on my Soul is how it feels: being scourged by angelic eyes, fierce with determination and Truth.

"No Regrets, Kind Sir."

I Seized her breast savagely; Lust flashed behind her eyes. And Always, as lightning Fades from stormy skies, only stark Reality lay before me.

* * * *

Second Position

"You love her." I nod.

It isn't that I expected her to mention Amy; this was a Point I expected not soon after our First Rut. That it comes now sets off all sorts of alarms in my head, but I won't Lie to Maiden and am actually *thankful* for the Sex-haze crushing any deception curled within my thoughts.

"Does she love you?" I hear the held breath, and answer as quickly as possible, yet smoothly, without malice or Emotion.

"If you ask me, I'll say this: I won't think for her. I'd like to think she at least gives a shit, but **LOVE...** no. And I've stopped Reading her; too painful." She nods quietly, chewing her bottom lips thoughtfully. *Did she Hear it?* "She's got The Normal Life. I'm something Different and Dangerous. I still can't quite get my head around how **quickly** I came to nearly destroying everything for her."

I open my mouth, the rant choking as Blind Rage leaps into every Thought. I suddenly **need** to be royally stoned. Maiden smiles softly, stroking my head tenderly; when she starts scratching, all Thoughts stop. I smile, thankful for the blessed silence inside my Mind. I roll over, gazing upon her features; they would be angelic, if Angels held steel in their Souls as she does; her Strength glows from within.

"Thank you."

"For what?" she chuckles. I shrug.

"It Needed to be Said, hun."

"So. Will you shave off the scruff for me? In exchange for... ' I chuckled softly.

I **did** Owe her.

* * * *

I'm Baked before shaving; bass rattles the floor as Rap fills the air: Hood Theme. Helps to soothe my Thoughts, guide them from depressed Thoughts about Amy and me. No shirt, just dark gray jogging pants, ankle-high socks and flip-flops... and a black rosary: Lounge Lizard Attire. Amy never liked this look for some reason. I brush off my black clippers and get to work, only slightly Aware of Maiden watching me. Even when I turn towards her, her Form is more Background Data. *She's FAST becoming Part of the Norm here; bad Sign.*

Then Hood becomes **Thug**; I Feel the Transition: Flow of Random Street Music; I could easily be cruisin' with Kilo through Da Hood. And when something swings the Mood into Lovey-Dovey Street Groove, the smile that slides across my Features... *FEELS* different until something Angry and Aggressive splits the air. Schizophrenic Street Flow: **Normal Me** before hittin' the Shadows, a Night Out-and-About... or just Vibin'.

I admire my ugly mug in the mirror, tossin' a good Screwface into the mirror when I'm done, making several passes over a few spots tucked away by the natural Light/Shadow within my bathroom... The White Room. She straightens when I sigh, finally satisfied, as she smiles.

"Nice."

"The goatee stays; don't like the baby-face Look." *Almost look HUMAN.*

"I dunno; I've always liked it: puts Wisdom in your eyes, Old Wolf."

"Shush." I swagger towards her. Smiling, she runs one hand through my goatee. I smile warmly, though. Amy used to do the same thing: complete with a smile drenched with Affection bordering on Love.

What Amy **never** understood: Big Easy Cook.

* * * *

Inside my bedroom I sit cross-legged in my black executive's chair. I'm keenly aware of the open window behind me as I cache my bowl. Mentally set to Write, I turn slightly: Maiden sways to my Street Beats. I raise one eyebrow, halting her momentarily; she continues after a few heartbeats, and I *examine* her, as I've done the dancers Working the Poles in Strip Clubs across America. She cannot Stripper-Dance, and I ponder stopping her attempts; as this turn into Training Thoughts I reach for my bowl and Blunt Station Zero.

"Take this as High Compliment: you're a horrible Stripper." I smile warmly before lowering my Gaze and taking a hit; I Focus on the Procedure, imagining Delta-9 working its mojo on my Thoughts as I feel muscles relax.

"I know; I can't dance."

"It ain't the dancin'; your eyes show you have a shitload of Humanity in your Soul; Strippers have precious little... if any; if they have it, they guard it like a Hustla guards his Money, ya 'eard? Just as valuable, if ya ask me." I get a hug, with plenty of tit-in-face; I lap at one nipple, thumb-packing my bowl with my left hand, tucking away the lighter in my right hand so it didn't touch her: Street Multi-Taskin' and O.G Respect of the Female Form!!

The music will soon hit Street Goth; Maiden has yet to see me like this within my Domain, and strangely, I'm more nervous about her seeing Hard Pimp Nigga than I ever was about the Demon Within. Why? Females like Maiden are Marks: either for their Money or Pussy, they are seen as part of the More-Money-than-Me Targets; this is Survival on the Streets: shit ain't pretty. So, naturally, I try to hide my hardening features from her, puffing long, slow and deep.

"Learn the Rhythm." I rise, drag her into a hug, then, letting my High swamp my Senses, bounce and rock to the Hip-Hop pulsating through the speakers. "Ride it; don't fight the Flow, hun."

She pulls me into the middle of the floor, pushing my chair away to make room; I miss her grabbing my cider, though when she takes a swig I Notice the look in her eyes. Grinning, I take a massive hit, blowing the smoke away from her after a Fourteen Second Hold-Time. Then we Dance: straight from Da Club Style.

Bump-and-Grind this ain't; strictly Get-Close-and-**TEASE!!!** She starts letting go, forgetting her hang-Ups. I let the music Flow through me as I watch this Beautiful Creature Dazzle me as she shrugs off inhibition; even those neck-to-neck sniffs were beyond Words; when I let my hands feather just over her shoulders she looked into my eyes, Enthralled. With only a Thought, I banish the harsh energy-

efficient halogen bulb, replacing it with Club
Shadows, smoke and Dazzle-neon
splitting/slicing those Shadows occasionally.

And then, for some strange Reason, the
tracks randomize, and I'm listening to Tech
N9ne; I slip easily into the darker Street Goth
Rhythms; so does she. She presses her body
against me and we rock off-rhythm; she opens
her mouth on the nape of my neck; I let the
Growl roll from my chest as I caressed her
back, the sensations: Sweet Bliss. She tastes
my flesh, the music soon forgotten as Passion
claims her Senses and Mine.

Only I don't stop moving to the music for a
bit; I time the song's ending to quick
movements, pulling away from her as my
fingers suddenly appear within her hair, poised
to Seize those locks; she gasps, eyes flashing.
Before she can react I've thrown her onto the
bed, letting my hands slide/guide her legs up.
SHE ensures they are spread wide enough to
let me see... ***MY FEAST.*** I yank her panties
aside *after* my hungry maw is filled with
feminine flesh; my tongue rams into her depths,
oblivious to the satin barrier save for rippling
just enough to savor whatever nectar dared rest
on its surface.

The Maiden and The Demon

An Urban Gothic Romance

* * * *

"Only a Gentleman..."

"I'm a Hard Man hun; Pimp beyond burial."

"So?" *There's that smile again...*

"So... only a Pimp can be a Gentleman, huh? Theory in the making?"

She snuggles into my arms; I *should change the Music. Later.*

* * * *

I hate hiding a Friendship; I hate looking into your eyes now; there is only cold distance, and the Lies are sharp ice shards blown by Cat-

5 Winds.

Won't do to pine away for you; you've made your Decision. So I move on, gathering the pieces as I attempt to let another inside. Only I'm doing this right beneath your gaze, and that means you get to see what you wanted: Nigga. I'll snag some Rebound Pussy or hit the Strip Club for a Quickie, shake off the Sex itch, clear my head and **then** *see to the emotional nightmare that we call Love... all while you watch. And you'll see failures... and if Fate wills it... success.*

And I can't allow myself any Thoughts about what this will do to you; can't even give Time to Think about you slamming my Choices, insulting them as Second Best or **anything.**

* * * *

"Is this when you stopped Reading her?" I nod, puffing my cigarillo thoughtfully as I pace behind her; strange to say, but allowing her access to the Blackened Journal is a bit more terrifying than I expected.

"You put everything into your Stories; I admire your courage." I snort.

"Courage? Write what you Know; that's the Rule. What I Know, just happens to be dark and twisted. Not sure how *many* readers I have because most of them lurk."

"Has she ever seen this?"

"**No**; that comes from the Blackened Journal, Maiden."

"Anything about me in there?"

"No; everything about you was Sacrificed to Katrina... at least until I get the hard drive restored: saved **that** just in case. Probably why Diary-X crashed: my attempt to cheat those Ladies out of my Works. Besides, that which is Priceless to me I keep within my Mind and Heart, where only they, I and God can

Reach."

"Eloquent."

"Truth."

"I know, Old Wolf."

"Not McScruff?" She chuckles softly, brushing her long locks with slow, even strokes as she continues reading.

"It fits you when you're like this. Oh... and I have to pee, Sir."

I chuckle, but she doesn't move until I nod moments later; I take my time gathering up my bowl and a lighter, fascinated by this Side of my oldest and dearest Friend.

"You do enjoy the White Room, My Dear."

"I do. May I ask Why **Meanstreak**?"

I forgive her lack of manners; this was a subject I did not want to share for many Reasons.

"Earned it in more than one Kitchen, Maiden; I am a hard Task Master within the Kitchen. Sometimes... too hard."

"And the Demon shows itself; forgive me for prying, Sir."

"Nothing to forgive, hun." We continue our discussion while she urinates; strange that its smell triggers Memories of strolls through the French Quarter and **not** the Nightmare Death-Caverns of the Superdome.

* * * *

"Malcolm!!!"

"Excuse me?" I blink. ***NAMES!!!***

"Malcolm McScruff." She smiles, extends one hand and strikes quite the Proper Pose, difficult to do with her black leggings pulled down around the toilet. Still, I take the hand and kiss it tenderly.

"You have me at a disadvantage."

I look at her, and when dark locks swam over her sandy hair, I notice a few glowing red hairs, some maroon... others true embers. I smile as the Name surfaced through my High; it parted respectfully, so I Knew it came from my Heart.

"Lady Rachel, I presume?"

She blushes; we don't laugh, though it shows in both faces; she giggles first.

"One Demerit?" She smiles.

REALITY CALLS

"Your cell, Sir." I glance at it... and frown;
Kilo doesn't call unless Biz.

"Show Tunes. Forgive me."

* * * *

Show Tunes: *Reality Demands Attention.*

"D; I need face-time, bro." Damn; not Baby
Mama Drama again. I sigh heavily, silently
cursing my adherence to Street Code: Fam
First.

"Swing thru; got Company, but you know
how we do, ya 'eard?"

"Oh *shit!!* Yo Lady... I forgot."

"Yeah. . but I Honor my Word, bro."

"Say... how much you Trust this one."

"Beyonc the Pale, bro."

"Oh... **HER!** She won't mind, then."

"Baby Mama again?"

"**MAN...** *FUCK YEAH!!!*" I chuckle.

"You said you wanted to know My Hood hun; get ready for Hood Education: *Baby Mama Drama.*"

* * * *

"Are you sure you wanna hear my Take?"

"Hit me, Bo." Kilo split the cigarillo deftly, tucking his folding blade into his hip pocket before dumping the guts into the trash.

"That baby ain't got your Name; financially there ain't no Strings. Your only issue: Morals." I emphasize my point: jabbing the blunt-roach at him, pausing, then offering him Last Kiss. He declines, shaking his head while indicating the Ghost Pile: blunt roaches from previous Session in Solace.

"And don't laugh; you don't know if you're Biological or not, but don't want **that** Demon hauntin' you. So... keep Yourself Ready as if that child's life may one Day rely on YOU."

"What about baby mama?"

"What about 'er? She fuckin' with ya Money? No? Leave her alone, then; no Slams, no snide remarks. I know how much silence Hurts: **trust me on that.** Keep Good Thoughts of her in your Head and Pray she is **MOTHER**, not baby mama. If she's stepped clear of your life, Honor her Wishes."

"Is that Your Way?"

"**It is *THE WAY*.**"

Kilo looked at me, **really** examining the set to my eyes, my posture; he was looking for Game... Playa; I'd like to think he saw **something**, but I'll be damned if I can accurately classify it. While only a few years separate us, I **FEEL** like the grizzled Ol' Coot in Da Hood when people Look at me that way.

And even though Kilo Breaks Bread, there is Lady Rachel's Presence; it keeps **both** of us On Edge and Alert. This is **pure** Male Ego/Street Law: **No Females Allowed in the Circle.** Kilo knows enough about me to Honor her Presence, however. In Street Terms: **she is My Ride-or-Die: the WOMAN who'll be with you no matter what.**

Not quite Right...

* * * *

"So **THAT** is Baby Mama Drama?" Rachel shook her head, completely amazed.

"Yep." I'm obliterated and stressed; Kilo's baby mama isn't the worst of the lot, but considering I went to High School with her, and *then* she seemed Normal, I'm more than a bit involved. Oh... I never **did** shit with her; we ran in different circles. Seems I made the Impression I assumed way back then: *He's a Strange Black Kid.* As to why hit me up: I Know a few things about the Shadows she haunts.

"Massage, M'Lord? You seem particularly troubled."

The Maiden and The Demon

An Urban Gothic Romance

"And coffee, Please? I Need to Think." I frowned as Thoughts snarled in my head; Lady Rachel moved gracefully, something I Noticed **only** because, at that Moment, such Movements clashed with the Thoughts/Feelings/Emotions shredding my Mind. When Clarity explodes within my chest, I sit up, turn the Hardcore down slightly, and Pour my Thoughts into the Scribble; Shape and Form will come later.

It is a full thirty minutes before I stop Writing. Before lying on my bed, stomach down and pillows tucked-and-fluffed, I place the ashtray on the floor along with bowl, black Bic lighter and half-blunt from Kilo's Session, all within easy reach. She brings me a fresh hard cider, placing it within comfortable reach. I'm ignoring the nagging itch/want for a blowjob because my neck and shoulders **really** need and *completely enjoy* Rachel's hands.

"No wonder you avoid black females, but they can't **all** be that bad, Sir." I breathe deeply before speaking.

"Not all are, but that particular Stereotype is rapidly becoming the Norm; that aggravates me to no end." I groan softly as she find a set of **very** tight muscles and focuses on them.

"I'm so used to fending **them** off I don't know *how* to React to the Stereotypical African American Female... you know... the Oprah Set..." She chuckles.

"Hey... Claire Huxtable... The President's Wife; that is the Stereotype so-called Normal African American today's Black Females aspire to... at least that's what the Media feeds us." I shrug, scowling slightly.

"Anything Wrong with that?"

"Not at all... but..." I sigh.

"Those are the *exact* Females I've been Taught as a **KID**: always beyond My Reach; I'm a Freak and not-that-Unique; know more than one Black Guy who reminds me of me **now...** and they're just breakin' Twenty-Somethin', hun. This... terrifies and concerns me." My gaze locks on the dying ember in my bowl, having just taken a hit.

"Who are *their* Role Models?"

"**Now** you're Seeing Thugs, Playa, gun-totin' parano'd Mean Mugs with platinum grills whippin' Donks and Pushin' Fat Whips."

I sit up, the Pleasure pushed back into its Hole; everything within me is Street Warrior right now; my High jerks into Street Groove. I vibe to the tures as I cache and reload. I inhale and exhale, both deep and sad.

"This is Street Law: Females are disposable to Hard Hearts runnin' The Streets, hun; not the Way God intended things, I'm sure; blame *that* shit on Money and greed. I've had a Black Female ask me what was **wrong** with me *because* I'm Clean: no Kids and no Charges. Pathetic... but in her Life, Clean Men are something God keeps tucked away from those like her."

"She liked you."

"I was interesting... a Novelty. I'd like to think she *eventually* came to Understand and respect some parts of Who and What I was back then, back in the Big Easy. Her Family is still in my Thoughts and Prayers." I empty my bowl and reload, my Thoughts filled with jazz-becoming-zydeco-becoming-something-completely-Different... yet **always** Alive.

"You deal with People... Individuals; Rare Breed indeed, Lord Alexander."

"I'm tired of the Baby Mama, Baby Daddy Cycle." Amy's image flashes in my Mind's Eye; my eyes narrow as Blind Rage explodes into a simmer. "I won't Rest until it's only a bad dream Mothers shush away from their frightened children. That means Men will have to resurface from the Nightmare Stereotype Reality and The Streets demand, and that takes **Honor**, Discipline and a bit of the Freak-in-

Home. It's complicated... *difficult* to Explain,
but I Know in my Heart it **must** Happen." Two
Flicks before Bless the Lungs: Street Cypher.
My Thoughts drift back and back and back
again...

*Desire Street... South Miro... The Wild and
Beautiful Bywater...*

"And you will be the Spearhead; you will
know First Blood, and make no Mistake,
Desmond..."

"I know; they've very nearly broken me
here... more than once." Sparking up, I inhale
slowly, mentally Feeling/Experiencing the
different THC levels nteract; my Thoughts
heave once, settling into quiet, purposeful Flow.
I leave my bed, switching Music to suit the
Mood Shift: Gothic Hood.

"You survived."

"It's what I'm **too damned** good at, and

damned tired of doing; wanna Live... and I'm Ready for the Long Fight: ***BUILT FOR DAT SHIT, YA EARD ME?!?!*** Too many want Temporary Feel-Good; that will never be Love, and until I draw my Last Breath..." Second Hit: inhale deeply, focusing on the slightly disturbing emptiness as Fresh-ish Air swirls around, the Sound eerily soothing despite its hollowness.

"What about the Army of Men like Kilo? They're looking for someone to Lead Them. Why not you?"

*She's over your Right Shoulder: Position of Trust. Listen to her Words, **but DO NOT Forget History.***

"Power; it will corrupt me beyond the crap, hun; I Know this."

"And you are ever Wary of the Power you Wield, m'Lord; this is a Good and Healthy thing."

I snort, shaking my head as my gaze

swings around the clutter on my computer desk; it helps block out the rush as Imagination conjures Images and Sounds... *unworthy*, though I don't know WHY that Word rings clarion. "Makes me Paranoid."

She hugs me, humming happily.

"Put to a Good Use, your Natural Paranoia?"

"Maybe." My Mood lightens, though the pending storm outside does little to help; its Power tickles Lust within us **both.** Her eyes flick to the parted blind, angry semi-sadness flashing every time the sun peeks out from behind unseen clouds.

"Heavy Burden: Leadership."

"Fit only for the Truly Strong." She hugs me close; her Confidence... makes me Smile as I caress her arms, my Thoughts slowly drifting from the Streets, settling into calm seas.

* * * *

Strength; she has real Strength; I'm
cunning and skillful; I am Observant and
Thoughtful; Strong requires serious definition.
Maiden splashes, reminding me of her
Presence while I work on Philosophy as the
Erotica dies once more, to my utter annoyance.
Why Write about Sex with such a beautiful
Woman nearby, **more** than willing to turn
Fantasy into passionate Reality? Yes, there is
the self-imposed Dead Line, and my Body and
Mind work best when Rested.

Why? Because the Words are swirling
around in my chest; no matter how hard I try I
cannot ignore the Need to Write; this is only
fueled by my Thoughts, the constant Data
Processing happening whether I'm aware of it
or completely oblivious. Even now I wonder
about Amy, even entertaining similarities
between her and Maiden. Easy to do when I'm
in this Mood: the Streets have taught me *never*
to Lie to myself, and I **am** the Missing Link
between them. Turning my Thoughts back to
my former lover squeezes my Heart, and I take
several Moments to Forget the Feelings for

Maiden, making breathing momentarily impossible; I'm slightly awed by the effort, and the snarling Demon that Saw this as One More Challenge.

"Both have their own Lives, and your Place ain't quite at their Side, Grimfang." My Words are low, bloated with Age and too many Scars on the Soul. *She is near...*

"Enjoy me while I'm here; I will do the same."

I swivel around to see her, cigarillo and lighter suddenly appear in my tilted head; sparking up... to avoid looking at her I force my Thoughts away from Amy, frowning as smoke gets into my eye **right** as Images of Amy's son rip across my Mind's Eye; something in *Rachel's* Tone: different... **deep** yet devoid of Seduction. And... There is a Sound, something you can't hear with the ears stuck to the side of the head.

"Trip Toys for Strip Club ambiance?" I

shrug, interested in finding out something. She changes the Subject every Time I seem close to a Great Truth or Dark Secret: a Thought I am only now beginning to recognize within the formlessness.

As she set things up, I found it easy to ignore her luscious thighs beneath the towel, though I **did** Notice how *easily* she moved through the cluttered Bachelor's mess; Strip Club is not something I've dropped over my Room frequently, so the **neatness** and arrangement... said much. Many good Memories tucked in the VIP Room and just squatting in front of the Main Stage, but too much Shadow Biz done in smoke-choked sleazy Strip Clubs back home in N'awlins for me to **want** her Triggering one of those paranoid-fueled Reactions.

"You've been waiting for this." I don't fight the impressed geek in my Tone; it hides the rapidly growing uneasy Street Warrior.

"Started planning this when I knew you liked Trip Toys. Wanna give me a hand?"

"Nah," I chuckle; we both like tech-tinkering, but I give her Time to fuss and fret over things, including loading a program to control the lights.

"Your system is far more advanced than it looks. Then again... it's You." She finishes, smiles, and struts to the light switch; Pride slams into Paranoia as I take a jaunty half-bow; she *Learns quickly.*

"Music, Mr. D.J.?"

"First... come sit wi' me, 'cher." I smile as the Mentality slides over me... easily. She turns off the lights, making her way easily by monitor glow. When she sits down, I pull the towel up, ignoring the dampness the instant my brain registers her Fresh-and-Clean flesh so close to my nostrils.

So imagine my surprise when she turns slightly, revealing my bowl and lighter and takes a hit; more... she passes me the bowl: Left Hand Side. Part of me, and part of her Image...

dies; instantly reborn as I envision a Black Woman doing the same thing, and got no such Reaction. Factored in Love; guess I still held Maiden as Pure; my *Presence taints everything around me.* I take a long, slow hit, pushing the depressing thoughts into blackest Nothing, ignoring the Howl ripping my rib cage. As I exhale she starts the music; when the screen fills with multi-colors the Light Show begins, and while it tickles the Raver Trip-Happy, the **MUSIC** rules the Mood, and that places me squarely within one of the Clubs on Cocaine Corner in the French Quarter; fresh from the Kitchen feelin' like I really need to burn off this Horn-Dog Aggression before I crash solo for another Night; between bills and trying to chase down my coke-addicted ex-roomie, not to mention Relationship problems and a Landlord siccing a fuckin' **Bounty Hunter** on my ass... I **NEED** to Fuck Me Sumthin': no Love... just Mad Monkey Sex and a smile in parting. No Diseases... No babies... No Attachments and **NO DRAMA!!!**

Then the music changes: a favorite Tech N9ne tune... perfect for the usual Endings to those Nights: So fucking Lonely. Temporary Pussy didn't scratch the itch: it made it worse... until the Moment Demon arose with a howling that tore through my entire body. I have never been afraid of myself until that Moment. And from then on, Alone has been, to me, the only possible Way.

She grooves, falling into the rhythm; I'm still enthralled by her Scent, but it can't shatter the Memories or their hold on my Soul, even as I carelessly stroke one arm. I try not to look at my bedroom door as Memory triggers paranoia, and the closed orifice shields Assassins seconds away from Raiding the Place.

"Thoughts, 'cher?" Not a complete Act, the Accent rolls lustfully, masking the Demon's deep, smooth breathing, this time Experienced **deep** within my Soul.

"Could you Make Love in the Strip Club?" The Demon barks laughter; I let the Neon driven shadows cover Street Amusement as I reply.

"It's *possible*, but I wouldn't bet on the Relationship where that happened."

"See... I couldn't; Stripping is a **JOB**; Work eventually gets on the nerves." I chuckle softly.

"What?"

"Nothin'; nothin' at all, sweetie." I snuggle close; she sighs happily curling into my chest as if to take a nap. The Trust Shown...

I kiss her head tenderly.

"Mood hasn't changed; this is Your Club, Sir."

"So the First VIP Room Christening comes..."

"From someone who Loves you more than they dare admit."

I stare at her head for a few heartbeats as I hear something *click* inside my head; I extend one finger towards her lips; she meets me, the Event slowly burning into my Mind as Time fades; the Room glows as she rises, dragging her face over my chest. I Feel the need to Scream out *I LOVE YOU...* but my body will not respond. Street Hard-Heart or Terrified Geek in front of an ***absolute SEDUCTRESS!!!!*** Doesn't matter; one look into her eyes tells me everything.

This is for US. She can't admit she Loves me, and even with everything we've done, **we have NOT Made Love**; even now, surrendering to Passion, she cannot deny Love's twisted Might. She **moves** like a Stripper in Love with me. Enthralled, not even the Demon can ignore her as she closes her eyes and sways, gripped by her own Demons. And... if Maiden perished with the weed smoke, Dame Rachel emerged from its smoke, fire and mist, illuminated by phantasmal Ghosts summoned by her graceful Power, admired by Fools and Foolish. Within that ravishing Body lay something Men dare Dream of, yet to say Possess... would cheapen it somehow. I rise, scooping her into my arms; she moves smoothly into my embrace, gazing into my eyes

without Fear. There is only Woman in my
arms... and I eye her as a Man eyes such
things: as a True Gentleman, one with Passion
most Primal... Compassion beyond Humanity...
Love Eternal.

* * * *

I seldom recall Dreams.

Do you Love her? Over and over again I
hear this Question asked, each time the Voice
is different. I don't quite ignore the familiar
ones: Mom, Dad, Grams. I stop and look for...

And I Feel it pulling me; I follow, but my
Right Hand aches, Feeling **empty** suddenly.

Do. You. Love. Her?

I am in a grotesque parody of Cocaine
Corner; a familiar blonde stripper strolls in front
of her pimp: guy with an Eight-Ball black

walking stick.

Focus; Do you Love her? The Voice mocks me... **and SOUNDS LIKE ME!!!** I look around, only slightly amazed to see a dark cavern lit by magma's red, sulfurous glow. I Sense more than see the Demon pointing one clawed appendage behind me, yet I am wary about turning around. Then I hear Maiden Scream; my Reaction is Instinct: Run *to her!!!*

I cannot breathe; running and breathing aren't synchronized.

Do you Love her? Anger flashes and I stumble, falling to thick red mud. I lift my head, though I see with the Demon's cruel, unholy Focus.

Do. You. Love. Her? My heart thunders; anticipation speeds my Sight through flashes of everything, until...

I wake up, inhaling the incense and Sex

Funk... **and In a Mood.**

DARKFYRE DAWN

Next Daylight: Out-and-about; Rachel has a silver vibrating egg nestled inside her sex during our trip to Wally-World. She doesn't quite blend in: her Capri slacks are stylish *without* Local Influence, and her sneakers are well-worn without grass stains. My usual day to Make Groceries, I'm a bit giddy: won't have to spend money and TIME on a cab to my Flop. She looks like Bummy-MILF, fitting in perfectly with every other semi-affluent White Female *Slummin'* in the place if she wore Stunna Shades. I'm just me. Fedora, jeans, Lugs... I finger my rosary, something that I Notice more than usual; slumped over the shopping cart, letting my eyes drift from the displays to everyone checking her out as I swagger along. That's when I spot her, the familiar movement barely visible through the clothes lining the aisle.

We went to school together. If we ran in the same circles, blame our Intelligence. I've always been Different, and *she* has always looked at me as if she's just seen a fresh pile of shit crawl from some pooch's ass, still steaming; never liked that look **or** the fake smile that always followed. Some things never change, and the instant she found out I'd survived Hurricane Katrina the Look gets Fake Pity tossed in; she even gives Rachel The Treatment. I sense Lady Rachel tense, pissed, but deferring to my Reaction.

And I'm *just* High enough to Start Shit. I look at her and imagine the bullshit slams Past and Present. She reads: Lurking Fan. *Ain't worth it; Keep Movin'.*

"We came from different Sides of the Track, and she won't let me or anyone like me Forget. Grates; fuels the drive to get out and Be Something Spectacular... only this place erodes the Soul of such Survivors, hun." We exchange Polite Fake Smiles; Rachel bows her head slightly, though Why I Notice eludes me.

"She's part of the Reason I bailed all those years ago, her and the ditbrains like her, and why I was more afraid of *surviving* Katrina: coming back **here.** Death is a Choice at times, 'cher." A Child squeals several aisles over to my right.

"She never knew you." Ever hear a hungry lioness behind a cage when she smells meat?

"Won't stop her from Judging me and finding me wanting. I wish I wouldn't let it bother me, but nearly *every* black female I've met **looks** at me like that. And I can't blame the shit I've been through, not even Katrina; I'm here; still hustlin'; still Grindin'. She doesn't Understand those Words; can't. She's used to a Life denied those without Connections and Legit Money... whatever THAT is. Once Money gets involved, something gets Sold. Me? NEVER Sell your Soul... and she and those like her have, to these Jaded Eyes, Lady Rachel. Straight Edge of the Gutta: Nigga tryin' **not** to Slip." *Fuck I need a Hit.*

"A Gentleman and a Scholar."

"Product of the Hood." I shrug, lifting the jug of cranberry juice into the gray basket.

"Take whatever you can *however* you can; I was just better at getting Knowledge and Wisdom than Home Invasions, though I've still **got** those Skillz; they come in handy."

As we enter the Electronics Department my gut jumps.

"Yo Demon!! What's cool wi' ya!"

"SPIKE!!!"

He flicks his gaze to Rachel; why I turn my head I cannot quite place to Pimp; still, vile, ichor-black-green Pride dared explode within me when she did not get Out of Pocket. I swag my gaze towards my Runnin' Mate; he is **completely** surprised, and Asks with one raised eyebrow. So I make it a point to **not** introduce her; when he jokes about my rudeness, she smiles politely.

"I'm Dame Rachel, a Life-Long Friend and ally of Lord Alexander." No accent, just a deep, warm Pride so unlike the twisted thing dying within me.

Now Spike is Pure Hood despite his sun-
tanned White Skin; Juggalo 'til he Dies, he
knows I'm a Dom. He's Fam, so when she
Addresses me Properly, he pulls back slightly,
eyes darting towards mine as he chokes down
any residual Game his Street Instincts demand.

"Yo... so... you're **HER.**"

I try not to smile; I also scramble to find
some Out that won't let her Answer.

She's close; I know... and surrender to her
embrace, sighing, a bit sadly.

Spike smiles, but he can't quite come to
grips with the Look pouring over my Features
as I briefly forget my surrounding and Know
Love.

"Well I..."

SHIT!

I raise my head, **PURE** Pimp ready to blast that bitch for opening her mouth and Blowing My Natural High; mouth wide open, I can see her drafting the gossip.

"M'Lord? Is there a problem?" Ever seen a hungry Lioness Scent **PREY?**

I look at Rachel; a cruel grin split her dazzling eyes. *Say...* **here's** *a New Weapon in my Arsenal against the Stupid, and Spike'll Back my Play 100.*

"Deal with her as you see fit, m'Lady. Spike?"

"Got ya back, Homie." We fade back and watch the Show, moving in Natural Tandem: Two Body Guards on Deck.

* * * *

We drop off the groceries. Unfortunately this Day requires my extended Presence in the Outside World during Daylight hours; doesn't explain why I allowed Rachel to rip that bitch a new asshole. I raise one eyebrow, remembering she didn't stop when Commanded: the silent vibrating egg suddenly leaping to life (I love tech toys!).

"Remind me to work on some system of buzzes, My Dear."

"Yes, Sir. I had difficulty figuring out what you Needed, Sir." *She enjoyed it... ENJOYED Defending you.*

"And you were getting a kick outta slamming her; she needed it. So did I, My Dear. Thank You."

"You are very welcome, Lord Malcolm."

I cock my head to one side, smiling at her ability to Address Me in-Mode without Thought.

"Next comes the Mall; not expecting to run into anyone I know there, unless a Lurker Outs themselves: highly unlikely."

I should learn to shut my fuckin' mouth: Kalla and her Ol' Lady were taking a stroll with their three year old son. Yes, you heard correctly. Kalla looks fabulous, but I figured: as vain as she is about her figure, birthing a Child would only deepen her Work-Out Ethic. Dee-Dee never liked me; she just **knew** I had a thing for Kalla, and she's right; Kalla is an *EXTREMLY* talented artist: oils are her particular favorite... or were the last time I checked her Facebook Portfolio. Now, I'm not concerned that Kalla will tell her Mother; from there, I loose track of the Gossip Loop. I **know** her mother lurks; Kalla let that slip the last time I fired off a message to her.

And I did not improve my standing with

Dee-Dee; Kalla is an avid Reader: a **fan** no less!! That means Rachel is a bit more than another White Woman on my arm to her.

"She'd be cute if she wasn't mad."

"Who... **DEE-DEE?!?!** Didn't think she was your type, Dame Rachel." She shrugs, chewing her bottom lip; thinking... *scheming!!!* "Do you still need One to Blab?"

"Only if I wanna be accepted in Normal Circle; what are you Planning?"

"Threesome." Simple, and I know more than one willing participant; each one I dismiss because they won't keep their mouths shut, which goes *against* having one female Talk about the Sex she had with me. Even so...

"Let me think on it."

Click. Threesome; didn't show up until she caught sight of Dee-Dee; I slice the short lesbian up into physical parts: Tits, legs, Overall Appearance: what you're supposed to do when figuring out What is Attractive; everything seems completely out-of-character for Rachel; **Maiden** is another matter, but even there: Reaching. Dee-Dee is big into SCA: the Society for Creative Anachronisms. Maiden and I dallied for a bit during our College Years, and the more I ponder them garbed in Ren-Fair gear, the more I dismiss Appearance, and begin to wonder: *What did you See in Dee-Dee's Soul, fair Maiden?*

* * * *

Each Day starts the same: Wake-and-Bake, tunes, coffee and a Black.

I hear her moan softly; I stare at the monitor, the blank document mirroring the White Noise quietly filtering into my head. No tunes; not in the Mood for them; my Thoughts churn, imperceptive beneath wind kissed blackness. Something within me settles on Classical Music, mere moments before she inhales.

"Morning, Sir."

"Morning My Dear; sleep well?" I turn my head towards her, the position forcing me to lower my head slightly; appearing to study her as a professor carefully watches a Student, something I find... *fitting*.

"Very; though I am a bit parched." Her Tone makes me smile.

"What can I get you to drink?"

"Your Seed, sir." I knew it; my smile brightens darkly.

"Bathe first, My Dearest; this is Your day, but I won't allow you to greet this Day smelling of last evening's Passion."

"***Desmond...***"

Her Tone shift isn't just dramatic; it lets me know precisely what's ahead. So I'm not surprised when a chat window opens... **from Amy**; for every Good Moment - Tragedy. Just one Word: Morning. The Smile jerks up one corner of my mouth as my Thoughts immediately seize upon Timing and Why. I Sense more than hear or see Maiden rise.

"Stay; this won't take long."

There is ruthless hardness within my Tone; though not intended to be a Command, the Force is there as my Will hardens, all Thoughts of Sexual Play twisting into dark, angry strands. Amy knew Maiden was in town; Kilo let that bit 'slip' during his brief chill-out. She also knows how much I truly Love Maiden; in Relationship Terms: Maiden is the only Female Amy truly *fears* taking me away from her. Amy also knows that Maiden and I are victims of Circumstance: given the **right set of conditions...**

That Thought makes me smile, though I check the Instinct to reach out and pull Rachel close.

"You gonna answer her?" She's pissed.

"Not yet."

Facebook is a wonderful thing; I know Amy Lurks there, so I post a Classic Cryptic Non-Comm message.

"Tell me your Thoughts, Maiden."

"She hurt you." Rage coils beneath her beautiful Voice; I nod, taking Note that Maiden does not mention *how* I was hurt. Broken Hearts are not rare, though Maiden and I have held each other up during some pretty bad ones... and those are nowhere **near** the full Dirt Pile.

"What do you Sense?"

Maiden touches my shoulder gently, warning me; I consider myself a natural Mentalist: interpreting Micro-Emotions comes easily for me. Maiden can do this as well, though she believes her intuition goes far beyond simple physical eyesight; I believe it, and have **GOOD REASON** to ask for her council on this, as my Heart and Mind are nowhere near aligned where Amy is concerned.

"Show me no Mercy, my dear."

"She wants to see me." I nod slowly.

Morning; how goes it.

Ok. You?

Up. You?

Doing the Wife-thing today.

chuckles Entertaining Company meself.

I hear. Enjoy.

You behave, sweetie!

"You paused."

"Pet name dangled at the end of my tongue for a bit." I flex my fingers and feel one eyebrow twitch; something in Rachel's Tone was shifting ever so slightly, searching for a **specific** Reply or Opening.

"She's angered you." Maiden starts massaging my shoulders.

"Not quite; I con't know where we stand. Sex fucked up that Friendship; a stark Reminder and Warning."

"Will it ruin **our** Friendship?"

I smile and chuckle, leaning back in my executive's chair. She spins me around, her face twisted by concern until she sees my eyes.

"Who else would we Trust with such Darkness, Lady Rachel?"

She smiles warmly, but I still catch her flicking an angry glance at the open chat window. As I move my lips to speak, the expression changes: odd amusement jerks a curiously twisted smile onto her lips.

"Looks like you are in high demand today, m'Lord." Crap; more Personal Shit?

"Who now?"

"Have a Look." Oh... **that** made me turn, slowly; Rachel's playful tone held *several* dark layers... and with good reason.

A request for Solace... one she knew I could not ignore.

"This is Interesting; I had planned on spending the Day with you, Lady. Yet this..."

"I *did* Request a Threesome, My Lord. Unless you feel..." I stop her with one raised hand, weighing the Pros and Cons, along with a very familiar *click-tick-tock* as I begin unconsciously preparing for something unexpected.

* * * *

Greetings; I am Honor Bound to Grant you Solace, Fair One.

Many thanks; I understand you have company, Sir. Forgive the Intrusion... but I

caught him cheating on me.

The Last Straw; your Motives?

Jedi.

chuckles

* * * *

"So you **did** Train someone; I wondered how much of that Story was bull; and Amy?" I watched something ghost over Rachel's features; it didn't ruin the beauty; it also triggered a very quiet alarm in my gut.

"Still doesn't have a clue; I shouldn't feel Proud of that." Hard **not** to smile, though; slightly amused at the Timing of everything, I closed everything down except for the music player.

"You did not Betray either of them; Noble... even when Doin' Dirt, Malcolm." She plants a gentle kiss on one scruffy cheek.

"She'll be here in an hour... and **you** are still thirsty, am I correct?" She smiled; I smiled... *tightly.*

There's a Street Saying that explains my hesitation at diving **fully** into loosing myself in her oral ministrations:

SLOW HEAD... GOTTA THINK.

ON BREATH AND TIMING

*This could go a million different ways, and those ain't even **half** of the Bad Shit going through my head. And the First Question: Why **now?!?!?***

*Call me paranoid; call it Knowing the Gossip Flow of this City **too** well; I expected her to get wind of Rachel's presence, but any meeting was slotted as Pure Chance. That **was** the case; with her catching her boyfriend Slippin' I figure things have to be **very** bad for her to even consider picking up Training again. Hell... she started training after he cheated the First Time: an Experiment in Rebound Sex that did exactly what I'd feared: unleashed the Sleeper.*

*Still... I just KNOW I'm missing something, and it has to do with Amy... **I Think**; the*

connection; *what's the Connection?*

I turn the Thought over and over in my head as I finally let my Focus include Rachel; she isn't looking up, but she senses the Shift, going from Soothing Blow-Job to satisfying **her** Craving. Time doesn't matter, and to be honest, I am something of an after-thought: nostrils flared, the only Thought: the Male Seed guarded by my rig d Member. I find my Thoughts leaving Paranoia as my orgasm approaches; I close my eyes as I **force** my Thoughts into Emptiness, basking in the Moment, burning it into memory as I caress her head with my Right Hand, she purrs; only **then** do we look at each other; the blend of Shameless Slut and shamed Woman-of-Breeding who *thoroughly enjoyed herself* is fascinating.

Time; there's about forty minutes before the Arrival. Plan. Plan. Think; something is Missing and it's preventing Pleasure from tickling the Mentals. Blaze: gotta See...

"Thank you, Sir."

"You're welcome; sorry I wasn't really here."

"Something troubles you about her arrival?" I nod; my features darken grimly as I mentally walk around the Unknown Information in my Thoughts.

"I'm missing something." I sigh, wet dick not even a minor annoyance.

"Take a hit; you'll figure it out." Shit... she does **not** sound happy; has good Reason to be mad as hell at me; can't shake the Feeling...

"Come, Lady Rachel; there is a Ritual I need your Assistance with."

*Hey... caught **her** off guard this time; wonder if that's a Good Thing.*

* * * *

She watches intently as I pour the rum into
the rocks glass; incense burns: three sticks;
one is Vanilla - Memory from the Past; one is
Dragon's Blood - Angel Guide my Steps. The
last I ask Lady Rachel to light, using one of the
black Bic lighters always within easy reach; as
she places it in the small glass candle holder I
kneel on the carpeted floor in my bedroom. No
Music graces the air, only the occasional low
breath as the heat warms the place.

I'm wearing a pair of black jogging pans,
ankle high socks with black toe and heel bands;
around my neck is my black rosary, cold upon
my chest. Normally worn over a tee shirt, even
in Summer, the Reason is as much personal as
Scientific; the hematite not only draws in body
heat, there is the **very** real Sensation of the
rosary drawing raw, vilest Evil from me.

"So, Wise One, Speak to me of Dark
Thoughts."

The Prayer swims into my Mind slowly;
though I'm breaking up a nice bowl-pack, there

isn't any **THOUGHT** given to the Action; there are no Street Thoughts, nothing save my pathetic Essence and God's Light tucked deep within my Soul: my Ember Within.

... and I shall Guide you through the Madness.

I mutter, "Amen," before bowing. I cross myself Properly, pack my bowl and, offering it and my Body's Suffering to God's Immeasurable Will, bow with Widow Maker high above my head.

The mood is shattered when Rachel gasps; eyes closed, I allow myself an amused grin: the rum is half-empty, and **neither of us touched it!!**

"Papa Ghede: he like 'is rum." The thick New Orleans Gutter-Creole Accent clung to my throat, slowly spreading over my glands; swallowing, I nod for the lighter.

* * * *

Smiles and introductions...

"Forgive the Timing, Lord Alexander; I have need of Solace, and am here to Resume Training."

"First... the break-up; do I get details... or was I correct?"

"You were indeed correct." The sigh pulls a sad smile to my lips, though there is nothing pleasurable about being right here.

"Sorry to hear about your wandering love," Rachel says gently, still somewhat shaken by the Supernatural happening.

"Nothing to be sorry about; he wanted something Slender-and-Blonde on his arm. **BLING**; and, as you said, Lord Alexander, my intended Role, as HE saw things: Financially Stable Housekeeper: also known as **LIVE-IN**

PUSSY!!!" My smile broadens; fool I Thought
as Rachel bristles visibly; doesn't take much to
know her *real* Thoughts about the sleazeball.

"And to answer the Question before you
ask: yes, Desmond, Amy and I spoke."

Rachel blinks; I nod, the smile flowing into
predatory territory as my rampant paranoia
does its Victory Dance... *uncomfortably, since
the Whole Story still hung on her lips.*

"She jokingly suggests that I, to use her
words, Seek Solace with you. She seems to
think it's a joke. That bothered me."

"Enough to want to prove her Wrong;
spiteful. Three Demerits, and I hope you do not
mind, but Lady Rachel here, may wish to
participate. She has never seen me Train; you
will be a Good Student today... I hope."

"I will do my best, Sir. I have never had
sex with another woman before."

"Not even a kiss, dear?" Rachel's **tone** jerks my eyebrow up; seriously bi-sexual, I've heard some of her College Tales, though I have **no** idea what she finds Physically attractive in another Female; more, there's that Searching Tone in her words, dangling as she helps bring in my arrival's things.

*Dark Minds Think alike; See how they examine each other, searching for **you** in the other.*

"Never, Lady.' She smiles softly, eyes fluttering as she tries to maintain Rachel's softening gaze; if you didn't Know the Local Females around here you'd think she was shy, **not** sizing up Competition... *which she WAS!*

"And this is but one issue before me; good thing God gave me two hands, since both of you like Spankings."

Cocky, but the idea swims to the surface

as I try to figure out just how much Amy knew about that three month window when she threw up every Wall to keep me out and I, pissed, gave her **all** of the space she wanted, ignoring her as I threw myself into Training My Little One.

    "**OOOhhhh... a SPANKING!!!!**" When *both* explode into giggles from the Monty Python reference, that annoying Void suddenly burps with pleasant amusement: Two Intelligent, funny Women...

    At my Disposal... Let's see what we Learn from this Encounter.

* * * *

    It is Training in the Presence of someone I Trust with my Life; in this, there is comfort. Still, I see no Reason to Break with Tradition.

    "Little One, you Know the Rules; get settled in quickly."

The Maiden and The Demon

An Urban Gothic Romance

"Yes, Sir." I make my way towards the front window, casting a quick glance at my Guest's hands; the action lingers for barely a breath as her fingers dance in our Silent Communication: *Wrong.*

* * * *

Rachel's Lesbian Experiences generally fall under College Drunk Nights; My Little One, Sasha, is a classic Country Girl despite her Big City Tendencies (intelligence, wisdom, **common sense**, something of a Short Fuse with Stupid); while not inclined towards Sexual Attraction for another Female, she has a very keen eye to what Males perceive as Attractive/Good Lookin', so she'll let her eyes slide over a Female body with the same *movement* as your average Swinging Dick, but no real interest... until Lady Rachel.

Both are here for My Attention; this is not lost on either female, nor am I surprised when The Stare Down melts into Sisterly Affection: neither wishes to irritate me during their initial

Meet. With My Little One Under, the Friendly atmosphere crashes into something cold and impersonal; Lady Rachel remains composed, but it is obvious: *she doesn't know her Role; good.* I cast a long look to the Outside World, my Thoughts barely registering the moving bodies. I have other Matters requiring my Focus, primarily... **What** was Wrong? I open the window for a moment, catching fresh air as I force my Senses to Feel everything... force myself to Notice everything.

What... was I missing?

* * * *

Sasha is, by Local Definition: a Good Girl; this means she isn't Sexually Promiscuous, PC for the Local Phraseology: *she ain't Easy.* From there, however, things get decidedly Dark, starting with Body Secrets.

Sasha becomes **very** wet when aroused, her nectar seemingly cranked out by the gallons... more if her breasts experience Pleasure/Pain. She enjoys breast bondage, and thrills at clothespins to the point where she actually knows where I keep several tucked away around my place, nothing out-of-the-ordinary in many old School African American Homes here: many still hang their clothes out on lines to dry. My gaze flicks to one such example nearly hidden beneath the fruit bowl sitting on the end table.

Sadly, Sasha has a problem I am discovering **many** Females today possess: the Need for Human Touch; not the actual hands-on-flesh; she, like many others, Male and Female, lack Physical manifestations of Love, Compassion, Attention and perhaps most importantly: **PASSION.** What she's gotten to date: the caress of Ownership... treatment like she was a Thing and **not** a Human Being with Feelings, Thoughts and Needs. And among the Needs: a Man who not only understands her, but Loves her because of/in spite of **everything!!!** Apparently recent Ex wanted, to use his Words: *someone Normal.*

"Have you been a Good Girl, Miss?"

"I lost my temper once today, Sir." She doesn't raise her voice more than necessary, and there is **no** reminder that I am already aware of her outburst. If anything, the Comment is Action-offered-for-Judgment.

"Aside from that necessity, have you been a Good Girl?"

"Yes, Sir."

"Very well; start Living Room Chores, please; there are matters I must discuss with Lady Rachel. You are aware of The Seal."

"I have not forgotten, Sir." She smiles, bowing slightly to us as she returns to the Guest Room; I keep the vacuum cleaner there, locked away with the other Toys/Supplies. I pivot, head into the kitchen and grab two hard ciders, removing the tops swiftly, without fanfare, show or hurry. I raise one eyebrow at Rachel as Sasha wheels the vacuum cleaner into the living room; Rachel eventually moves towards my bedroom door, but she pauses at the entrance.

"You hear correctly, Lady Rachel." My words slip over her shoulders. "She does indeed have a vibrator within her." I nudge Rachel into my room, closing the door quietly.

* * * *

"Good Girl?"

"It means has she adhered to Local Standards when getting off; while she does enjoy sex, her Sex Drive is about as high as my own. So once the Doors close, Good Girl becomes Sex Fiend, at least as far as Locals are concerned. You two are alike in this: both of you adore Coming Home to a Twisted Love. *Speaking* of which: you need a Drink." Towel covering the chilly synthetic leather seat I drop my jogging pants rather unceremoniously and take a seat.

"You're Thinking, m'Lord; something troubles you about her visit?"

"Not particularly; doing my best to Forget the Paranoid Street Nigga screaming in my head right now," I sigh, stretching my neck; I smirk at the wound-rebar sound, the motion flowing into painful wince. *The only real difference is Location: Where their Hearts Are...*

"Then allow me..." I smile thankfully; good*... she bought it.*

I force myself to forget the Streets, and I **Notice**: Lady Rachel, sucking my dick, does not at **all** attempt to distract me from Thinking. She never looks at me unless I actually stare at her, my Thoughts Focus on Sex-induced euphoria instead of elsewhere, and I'm not at all surprised when I start shrinking as the **NEED** to Blow a Load down her Throat slowly evaporates; deep within the back of my skull I hear it, the slithering grown black beyond black as one Word explodes in my Mind; LOVE**.**

Yes, I Love Lady Rachel; will always Love her. It bothers me that the Demon wakes, and I cannot blame Sasha's presence or the blowjob.

It Senses Tomorrow, and the Stress annoys it enough that the Scent of Love and Passion parts like a mist, revealing Amy's smug expression.

You Love with Passion; now Feast with equal Passion. There will be Time enough to sort through this madness.

* * * *

Hey: Why are you being Stupid? And Why ain't Rachel?

I blink. Yep; that's what was gnawing at me; I'd watched Sasha enter, eyed her Dress Code and did **not** React; Status Quo for her, she would have to change before getting to her Chores. I was with her when she went into the sex stores to purchase the pieces. She had great poise. So much that the clerks **knew** she was a Newbie with a Wild Side: **Status Quo.** That meant I wasn't boyfriend, but the Gay Black Guy many White Females have; another Local Custom it seems (One Token Gay Black

Male, one Token Lesbian: Friends of the Alternative Set).

Stupid. Sasha is a Vibrant Woman, young only by years. The Passion boiling within her hasn't even reached a full simmer, its present persistence only *hints* at the Creature a mere seven or more years will unleash.

Discard the Notions of Man; See with the Soul... that I may Feast well this eve.

Eyes lower, resting the gaze upon Lady Rachel; yet somewhere in the back of my head, the Demon looks over *its* shoulder, Focusing... misty gray Thoughts.

"Tell me you Love me, Desmond." Once stroking my member, she releases me, her head slowly rising; something screams at me, a Strong Male voice filled with terror; I met oblivion eyes wide.

"Why now?" Unholy power surges through me.

Better... Calm... Good...

"Because I'm afraid she will say what I... Need."

My right hand twitches as she creeps closer and closer to me; I hear someone scrambling inside my head as she opens her eyes; Emotions hold her Soul. My own: a sphere made of Void.

I Seize her head violently, my Right Hand moving before **any** Thought... any Human Thought; my blood is white-hot plasma, yet my flesh: I Feel Cold Winds swirling through the hairs on my arms... between the ridges of finger and palm prints; I can only hear a high-pitched whine in my ears. Rachel digs her hands into my chest, her face horridly twisted by primal, savage Lust... and the last shreds of Humanity familiar to me... because once I called that Place: **HOME**.

"Our Love is Eternal, Old Wolf."

* * * *

I open the door to my bedroom; Sasha was just finishing vacuuming the floor, turning slightly to acknowledge my appearance.

Now... Love Consummated... what to do with this? I let my gaze drift around the living room, nodding slightly: as usual - Everything in Order.

I wanted... **NEEDED...** a Long Shower, followed by a Work Out; my head wasn't clear despite the **AWESOME** Love Making.

Demons Making Love. My gut doesn't twist into knots at thinking of Lady Rachel as a Demon. Like all Ladies, she holds **many** Demons within her stately, graceful form. I glance at the floor; Sasha faces me fully, waiting patiently.

"Clean me, Miss."

"Right away, Sir."

"And once you are done, Lady Rachel rests on my bed; Clean her as well."

"Of course, Sir," she smiles. She enjoys the taste Rachel's copious fluids leaves on my dick, and some part of me ticks away another Story Hook; as she dries me off with her tits, I cough once.

"Enough; crawl into my Room and see to Lady Rachel, Miss."

Lady Rachel is mistaken; there is no Love within this one. You Know the Term...

99.9%; Sasha is perhaps one of the *few* Souls I actually consider Friend in this Town; this Sliver of Thought sparks others; a deep chuckle resounds softly in my Mind as she makes her way into my bedroom. While there may be Physical and Emotional *Connections*; there is no True Love. **BULLSHIT!** So... we jest as Locals do: Siblings; that makes our actions Interracial Incest, a common hushed occurrence in the area, and a nice, Twisted Joke.

To be strictly sensible: this is Stress Relief for her; Sasha is a very Good Girl who just happens to be a Slut-at-Heart; when it comes to Sex, simple Dick-in-Pussy will not suffice. Then again Good Girls, at least according to Locals Standards, do not wear tight denim mini-skirts; they do not purr happily when I pull up said skirt caressing both pale globes casually as I ponder What to Do to this beautiful Creature.

Plans must be made; she will leave you soon, and then...

Reality; thoughts of Amy flare in my head, followed immediately by aching shoulders, the only part of me that actually *hurts*; otherwise I am actually rather energetic, though the **direction** those Energies are about to take me will probably drain me. **If I participated as Dick**; I cock my head, frowning as I did not hear pleasurable moans bubbling from my room, and Lady Rachel tends to be rather vocal when being eaten. *Has your Pupil Failed you?*

WHAT SHADOWS TEACH

Lady Rachel lay on my bed; Sasha waited
on her knees at the foot of the bed, hands
folded neatly on her lap.

"I didn't want her to start without you,"
Rachel coos; I raise one eyebrow silently,
offering her a glass of orange juice. She rises
up on her elbows, accepting the drink. We
toast, and as I, smiling warmly, caress the left
side of Sasha's hair; Sasha doesn't respond
visibly; I hide my Reaction to her subtle
appreciating by taking a swallow from my drink.

"Proceed, Miss; though before you do,
Why did you Obey Lady Rachel?"

I do not Train silly little girls; she is highly
intelligent, rivaling my own natural Micro-

Emotion/hyper observant paranoia.

"She called you 'Malcolm.' It is a Name I
have not heard you called before, and I
Hesitated, Sir."

"I told her I gave you that Name."

And Names have Power.

"Names have Power," Miss intoned
solemnly. Rachel raised one eyebrow, her
eyes asking several Questions.

"No Secrets here, Lady." *Note to Self:
Sasha's Runnin' Game.*

"You are aware he is Voudoun then,
Dear?"

"I know much about Sir; **you** are the Shield

Maiden, he is Blood Brother One."

She doesn't chuckle; Sasha knows and respects the Tale behind those Names, yet it is the flatness upon which her Tone vibrates lively that I take Notice of; Sasha doesn't give me grief about my Street Habits, and has become rather adept at Street Code and Silent Speech. When I began Teaching her, I questioned my Logic. Now...

Guard yourself, m'Lord; there is Danger here.

I remove my hand; Sasha sets to her Task as I sip my OJ, posting up against the door jam: Watching and Thinking.

* * * *

Both Women are in the living room, enjoying Down Time and each other's company; I sit cross-legged in my executive's chair, a hot cup of coffee quietly cooling on my cluttered computer desk. I clear the ash from my bowl before taking another slow pull, holding the smoke fourteen seconds (Cypher Rule); I exhale slowly, my Thoughts suddenly mired in Delta-9 sludge; this is a Good Thing, as an Idea is beginning to drop Puzzle pieces into place.

Sasha is a Student; she is not my First, just my most successful. She is also... a Mistake: our Friendship began from our Love of Writing (she's a Poet!!). I let my gaze wander over the Journal Entry burning into the monitor; I frown up as **again**... the only Faces that greet my Mind's Eye are Amy's... **and Lady Rachel.** I flip the partial cigarillo between my lips, fire it up and begin the spitfire staccato typing that accompanies what I laughingly Term: Brain Drain. I stop after writing *kunoichi*, take a few moments to research the legendary Female Assassins... and discover the ***onna-bugeisha***: the **PROPER** Japanese Woman-of-Breeding and *skilled* Warrior. The soft knock on my door doesn't catch me off guard: I Think of Sasha upon reading of the onna-bugeisha, so I **know** who is there despite the apparent lapse in being Aware of my Surroundings: nothing is further from the Truth.

Case in point: My door doesn't **budge** until I turn my music down, acknowledging the Soul on the other side. Rachel: she'd be at my side by now. Sasha is a Good Girl: Respectful and well Trained.

"Begging pardon for disturbing you, Sir." She averts her gaze; everything Sasha did: Perfect *Servant*. When I Feel Rachel peeking around the corner, I Know.

"Please... and bring Lady Rachel, Miss Sasha."

"Right away, Sir." I catch her respectful bow and nod stiffly, yet before closing my bedroom door, leaving a small crack, I see a very familiar smirk tugging at her lips; it takes two heartbeats before it strikes me.

I am quietly preparing not only for Rachel's eventual exodus, but the Nightmare I foresee afterwards.

Boy... there's a Demon inside of you with a

Meanstreak ten miles wide...

"My Lord?"

"I've decided to start Looking again."

"If I may... you do not have to Look Far, Malcolm." Rachel's smile is soft, but I cannot Trust it: she called me Malcolm. Sasha Notices the name Change, barely managing to keep her gaze squarely focused on Nothing-in-Particular: Street Samurai Trick, something else I helped her *refine.* So... Sasha **knows**: Rachel **meant** *HER!!!*

"True, but there are... Local considerations to address; Sasha?"

"The second he starts lookin' for His Other Half he's gonna get swamped with some pretty foul waters; not a lot to choose from here, on either side of the pool." Local dialect, her Natural Charm shines through, but does **not** flicker in her body's polite stillness.

"That... and considering what's Out about me, I would not be surprised if a few sought Side Action Training."

"You would have Playthings, but I Sense you find something *particularly* unsettling about that." Only Lady Rachel's Tone tickled Thoughts of Amy.

"Some of the places I must go..." I smile, the action dripping Big Sleazy as I turn over several Puzzle pieces carefully, Thought-Conversatin' with myself as I try to make sense of the two Missing Pieces that I know lay in the near Future. I blink suddenly.

"Council." Sasha immediately turns and leaves my bedroom; Rachel stammers, slightly shocked, I explain quickly.

"I have Need of her wisdom and intelligence; Comes at a Price..." I chuckle, the smile softening and warming as Sasha returns: jogging pants and a white, over-sized tee shirt; the white rosary around her neck is touching: a

Reminder of something we share. She also has a book, and curls up beside my chair, adjusting herself easily, though she does chuckle while moving my work boots aside.

"They still need to be polished; Who?"

"Joyce; three years and her divorce still stings; only made worse because I won't sleep with her."

"Hey... she **is** a year older than your mother."

"Really, Malcolm?" Lady Rachel chuckles; I don't need to see Sasha's expression, as I'm trying **hard** to forget having someone two years older than my mother jack-off my arm between her tits *ACCIDENTALLY!!!*

"Oh yeah; and its two years, hun." I sigh, a slight chuckle rasping beneath my words as I stroke Sasha's hair.

"I've got something planned to compensate for her, but what I **really** Need..." Sasha taps her right foot on the carpet twice.

"Someone to smooth things over when you start acting..."

"Almost, Rachel; you're Coming Out as a Dom at Work... aren't you." Sasha turns towards me, narrowing her eyes as if concerned; I smile softly: the slight twitch to her right eye always makes her look impishly cute.

"Yeah...; the place is packed with Freaks: Closet and Flirting-with-Freak; hit, anyone?"

"Cypher, Sir?"

"Rachel... you're technically to my left... so..." She reaches for the folding chair in my closet; Sasha adjusts herself slightly as I scratch the base of her neck, just below the hair line.

"My Pleasure."   She takes First hit -
Green Hit; I chuckle as her Rookie Cough
shatters Seasoned Smoker Façade, and raise
one eyebrow at Sasha's Professional Hit.
*Lighter in Right Hand, Mysteries in the Left;
brush away bangs: Clear Sight is best. Inhale.
Exhale. Flick Twice, get comfortable; tilt the
head Thoughtfully; Consider oblivion as the
Lungs fill with Smoke.*

"Been practicing?"

"He wondered where his stash was going;
took a page from your book: Smoke and Think.
Worked." She places the black Bic lighter over
the glass spoon, handing both with her right
hand, head-first.

"Think like the Enemy." I shake my head
as I glance down at the angelic features,
scowled up because of the dark, troublesome
Thoughts flowing across those dark eyes.

"He wasn't worth your Time, Sister." *At least her concern is Genuine; this is **really** beginning to get out of hand.*

"I know," Sasha sighs. I cough, but only because of a few Thoughts that bubble up through my High; I marvel at their shimmering illumination before my High settles around my kidneys and lower back.

"When you Train...; you won't go for the Trappings?"

"Not unless the Student wants to experiment and finds them pleasing or Necessary," I state, my gaze darting across the sci-fi Tale I'd opened the instant after Sasha first knocked; I cock my head to one side and bang out a few paragraphs.

"Music?"

"Your choice," I say, **oblivious** to the

Speaker as the Ideas flow from my fingers easily, the staccato beat perfect.

"The Forgotten." Sasha; I pause, nod and set the Playlist for Random before diving into a different Tale-Series: something... befitting my Mood.

* * * *

It isn't important that you be submissive; it is **VITALLY IMPORTANT YOU UNDERSTAND:** *I am a Dom. This does not guarantee you Restraint or anything from the Standard View of The Lifestyle; it does not guarantee* **I** *will even attempt to lure you Down the Rabbit Hole.*

So the Question becomes: **How does a Woman go about getting The Freak?** *Asking is out of the Question as a Matter of Social Norm, though it is the Precise Answer: Ask. This is My Logic:*

You are **not** asking me for part of me: **You are Questioning your Personal Limits sexually, and Trust me to do two things: Control Myself and keep you Safe.**

I Guarantee Self-Control; I Guarantee to Guide, but Know this: **the Decisions are Yours alone.**

I pause, the Thought Incomplete, yet this does not upset me; satisfied for the moment I close the document, revealing another.

* * * *

You really **are** *an odd One; no wonder you've been single for so long.*

Gee... THANKS.

I MEAN THAT IN A GOOD WAY; SAVED YOU FOR...

For who?

Someone Special.

She turns, and once more I see through
Botticelli's eyes; I blink as Sasha playfully slaps
Rachel's face with my dick; I gaze at reality,
the Dream-Memory/High-Illusion gently fading;
I chuckle softly before lifting my glass bowl to
my lips.

*Hedonistic... Roman-Style pleasure; no
wonder the Civilization crumbled if this was the
norm for those With Money. Ya think mankind
would figure this shit out. But... greed got
passed along after the Plague, I guess; Proof:
Gene Pool needs a massive chlorine
treatment... STAT.*

"Snuggle," I sign, the Command greeted by
coos and seductive sighs as both Women
slither up my reclined body.

Music: Hardcore; two naked Women

snuggled lovingly beneath either arm, blazed outta my mind and puffin' like two Dragons: close to The Rapper Lifestyle; I suppress the sarcastic chuckle: the comparison is utterly wrong.

Sasha and Rachel are Cuddle Whores; that Cuddling often degenerates into Sex is inevitable, **but NOT the Goal**; they are **Women**, not Things or Toys, and *certainly **NOT** Pussy-of-the-Moment.* And, according to the Rap Image, there should be Goons loungin' around outside, armed with Street Banger Specials; I'm **also filthy stinkin' rich from some illegal venture.** Sorry: hard workin' Broke Nigga Strugglin' here; that is Why my Smart Phone isn't State-of-the-Fashion-Industry, the display constantly flashing as Ho, Model, Nigga and God blows me up, and Why my flop doesn't see a constant parade of Silly Hoes: I'm a Baller-on-a-Budget.

"They won't understand the Change." Mentally flipping through images, I allow my Thoughts to float upon the comfortable presences next to me. Story Ideas, paragraphs and conversations fade, becoming muted White Noise.

"I'll be there to help on this end; Why the worry? Amy?"

"Trust your Instincts, Desmond Alexander Mathers; they are never Wrong and you Know it."

"Sis? Why the name switch?"

"He Knows Why," she sighs, **content** in her confident Statement.

High; missing the Obvious... so Chill and let it stew; Sasha moves slightly, taking a breath much deeper than necessary.

"Start with a Black Female," Sasha sighs; I remember Keshan, yet *dismiss* considering her for this particular Task.

"If I can find one." I start to chuckle, but

something strange happens with my Thoughts;
not quite a snarl, but several Images snap into
focus, and I cannot *quite* dismiss them. And
each one reminds me of Rachel: My Maiden.
Dead Things...?

"If they believe they will Know Solace
within your Domain, they will come, pardon the
pun." Again Rachel sighs, only there is lustful
boredom dangling at the end, a whimpering
thing; that's when the snarl uncurls, several
pops resounding inside my head as memories
rekindle; not **all** of my Tales were Sacrificed to
Hurricane Katrina's watery embrace and one
surfaces from those brackish waters.

"I never told you the end of that Story..."

"She got pregnant... didn't she?" Rachel
mounts me, and it is then that my gaze shifts.
Sasha now kneels by the bed, and even though
she is naked, I **SEE** an Angel in White; I also
see a robed female: Japanese, quietly waiting
for Orders from her Lord.

"He left me because I would not bear him a

Child; I would not, because I decided on the Day I laid eyes on you that **only** you would Father... **FATHER...** My offspring. Dally as long as you want, My Dark Priest; I will always Love you, and Know you will always be a kind and loving Father... beyond Trusted."

Yes we're high; doesn't matter: she's gotten tired of keeping things pent up. Back then she called me her Dark Father Confessor, something I had to explain to Sasha when she did the same thing and I exploded: fresh from Katrina's Fury, everything was raw and exposed, **especially** my Emotions. We make Love; Sasha witnesses what I will never give her, and part of me wants to watch her Reaction... Know her Thoughts.

Yep; I'm not completely In the Mood, but I have some damn good Reasons for this. Rachel would never regret getting pregnant by me, but she isn't the type to get stoned and be Stupid... *and I don't see that in her eyes.* I don't see some desperate attempt to snare me: I See the Thing that fascinated me and terrified me the first Time I ever Dommed out on an experienced submissive.

If you watch carefully, something primal
and Savage flickers over Features that are
cruel, cold, desperately innocent, and **HUMAN**;
I blink mentally, shaking an invisible head as I
come to a chilling Understanding; whether Fact
or Fiction, before me now is the Reality: she
will be the Mother of My Children. She's
foolish for this, and I am no less a Fool for
letting it happen while we're baked.

We shall see how this Plays Out; Game...
or Truth.

Curious that it feels almost good to be
taking this Risk; I think about Sasha, and while
Rachel basks in her Moment, I get the very real
sense that Sasha wasn't watching me Make
Love despite Feeling her steady gaze during
the Event. When she finally makes full eye
contact, I knit my brow faintly; she replies:
barely moving her head, her feather fall sad
Smile flickers at one corner of her lips.

* * * *

Rachel is in the bathroom; Sasha, seated in my chair, taps her knee twice, silently.

"Speak."

"There's a But." I nod, placing the glass bowl back in its place on my desk.

"Oath." Sasha nods, another Piece clicks quietly into place and I frown slightly.

* * * *

Sasha let her gaze drift from the laptop monitor to Lady Rachel's sleeping form.

She's got it set in her head that a Kid will keep you.

How certain...

She told me as much; don't trust a Woman's Instincts?

She allows herself a cautious smile; Desmond trusts her with his Life. Lady Rachel also falls under this umbrella, but she's seen one too many Females burn up a Good Men; unless God tells her otherwise: Desmond Alexander Mathers **is** one of the few Good **MEN** walking.

She watches Rachel roll over, placing her back to Sasha; swiftly she minimizes the online game and opens the word processor program, her eyes flicking to the list of previously opened documents; all *from his Private Journal: witch...*; while the laptop had the right access, Sasha fumed silently at the invasion.

*Well now; seems you **copied something...***

* * * *

From the Blackened Journal

Way of Balance - 0420

"What if he were your Child?"

"I'd do Right by him; Words... and the Truth, but we'll never know, will we?"

"Why are you so *cold* to me?"

* * * *

Amy... you broke my Heart; I had more than a hand in that debacle, but make no mistake: Loving you Hurt in Ways I knew would linger. That's Why I hoped you would **stop** my stupid ass... Why I was afraid you'd fall for me. I did not expect to become Poison within your Mind: a venomous Idea.

And the Silence; it felt like Pulling TEETH just getting you to open up; I'm difficult, but

that's because I Know the Demon Inside me.
You have yours; everyone has 'em. Easier to
Deal with them if you have someone you
Trust... Love... Care about; I guess that wasn't
me. Been *guessing* too damned much, so I'll
honor your silent wish and stop.

I dismiss the Sex. What I miss more than
anything is the Friendship; that off-the-wall,
brutally Honest Flower; now just a desolate
plain... wind-swept and barren. **And I don't
know where or when this shit happened!!**
One day I looked at you, and a pit opened in
my Soul; to Know that I am poison to you... that
by being your friend I risk *destroying* everything
you've struggled for.

Yeah... and I'm supposed to smile and be
friendly; tell me how. Tell me I shouldn't be
dead, drowned by depression and negative
Thoughts; tell me how to avoid the agony
tormenting my Dreams.

When you wondered who the Father was,
you looked at me as if you expected me to Go
Hard-Headed Nigga and leave you high-and-
dry to deal with whatever happened. Damn... it
tore me apart: you acted like you didn't believe

I Loved you; and the Silence; no Friendly banter... just avoidance and stares. And what did I do?

Tried to figure out one thing: how much do you Know about me?

Do I matter?

If he was Mine I'd do Right by the Child and you; it isn't Words; to me, the Right Thing I **will** do; won't be easy, but nothing worth having comes cheap. What worries me is whether or not you expected me to tell you to abort. **It is a Living Being... and Reasons/Excuses be damned: it is Murder, pure and simple.** And yes... I am heartless enough to back you if that is your Choice; it will not diminish my Love for you, but the Taint of Murder lingers no matter what anyone may say: Taking a Life Changes the Soul. That said: the Choice is Yours, and I'll follow you through the Gates of Hell and back.

But I guess you don't believe someone can

be that stupid; guess again, hun. I'm not a paycheck. Not a Fool. Just one Man with a Dream and the Drive to see it done. May the winds guide you favorably as you Travel, Amy.

* * * *

"Time, hun; we're still connected." I swallow, choking back the tsunami.

"I can't. And you know..."

"Not a damned thing, sweetheart," I chuckle softly.

"Why do you still Love me, Desmond?"

"Love is Eternal; don't blame me for Playing by the Rules." I smile, flip my fedora on, Pimp lean proud and natural; I don't kiss her, but by all that is... the **MOMENT** lingered.

I walked away that Day; by Street Law I did **damned** Good; Like Mike said: *the kid is not my son!!!* Street Nigga/Thug Law sez Click-Out on da Bitch and bounce: Old Pussy.

What it doesn't say a damned thing about are the Thoughts still flying through my Mind: Questions screaming to be Asked, **DEMANDING** Answers. I remember listening to the door close silently behind me, symbolic of our Relationship on so many levels; Painful Memories of Foolish Decisions. Street Law doesn't have any Rules for Loving someone who either can't or won't Love me back; doesn't cover the Fear and loathing I've seen behind your eyes every time you look my way.

All I Hear from the Streets: *she bailed because you're BROKE!!!* She's terrified you'll be Just Another Worthless Nigga. She doesn't Know You... or is terrified of Knowing you; doesn't matter: **she made her Choice; Go-Time, Hustla.** ***Go get 'em!!***

Ya got Played; dust ya shoulders off and get back in there!!

* * * *

Ah... now you make some Sense, Lady Rachel; she closes the word processor, loads a bot for her online game and types silently, Requesting an Audience; the chat window, set on silent, flashes: *one more blink in the ether* Sasha smiled, the glow illuminating the rapid Thoughts flowing over her surprisingly stern-set features. She doesn't look at Rachel as she slips shadow-like from the room, merely extends her hearing until she Notices Rachel's deep, even breathing as she dreams.

Stay the curse swelling in your Thoughts, Bushi.

She pauses; her eyes moves slowly towards what little of Rachel she can see, ignoring the night-draped darkness and the cluttered Home it conceals from the unknowing. *Behind me... in his Room*; Sasha inhaled the scant details as she swiftly makes her way into Desmond's room, carefully twisting the door knob instinctively, only dimly aware that the rapid-fire staccato from another long Night of

Writing as it rips into the semi-silent air, the hiss from the ancient heater as it spewed warmth into his Home: pale company, quickly swallowed by the dark shadows.

She smiles at the site of the small bottle of sake resting on his computer desk. He nods once, a gentle smile playfully tugging at his lips as she closes the door behind her.

The Seal is Set.

* * * *

Her Last Night here; she's outside, face held high as the wind whips the maple leaves across the grass; air smells like heavy rain, though full-blown Storm isn't quite there: not enough angry-electricity ripping through the atmosphere. That... and it's a touch too damp for...

"Desmond?"

"What's up?"

"You will never leave my side, no matter how foolish I am, correct?" She sounds controlled; I know better.

"Always. Though you're gonna regret that when I die: Voudoun... remember?"

"Gonna give me a charm to raise you from your Grave?" She isn't quite sure about how much Joke is within her Words; I don't give her Details about my chosen Religion and she's never bothered to ask for specifics.

"If you Hurt... I'll know and come to ease the Pain." I shrug, twisting my lips up at the urge to blaze during the Autumn Night.

* * * *

"She is misguided." I nod slowly.

"M'Lord... she would Mother your Children, but she cannot be with you. She believes..."

"That she can correct the damage done by Amy and the others."

"You are not done with Amy, not yet." I hear the Storm approaching in Sasha's words.

"In Matters of My Heart, I fear I am indeed Too Close to See properly; I've contacted Dallas." Sasha nods, pleased.

"He is a scoundrel, but his Loyalty is without Question."

"Second only to your own, Little One; you're planning to betray your Oath with her." Sasha's eyes go wide for all of two seconds.

"My Lord Follows a Code. I Follow My Lord."

"Blindly?"

"M'Lord does not have Blind Eyes at his side, only Focused and Driven Souls."

"Sasha? Why? Why me?"

* * * *

"How did you meet Sasha?" *Here it comes...*

"At work, though not where I work currently; remember when I told you about getting fired?" Rachel nods as she swallows the medium filet mignon. "She approached me afterwards; it was supposed to be Get-Drunk-and-Fuck. Unfortunately..." I can't resist the smile as I recall that cold January Night.

"Your Code prevented it; Honor First; it's a wonder she didn't fall for you then and there," she chuckles, though the sound reverberates with fearful undertones.

* * * *

"Bret." One Word; one Name; my lips twitch as memories suddenly dive into a pit of infinite, unholy Dark Thoughts.

Her ex-boyfriend used The Lifestyle as Game; he played with her emotions and nearly choked the beautiful Woman before me now with his childish temper and utter lack of self-esteem/respect. When I first saw him he decided it was a Good Idea to *Get Swole*: puff up his chest and stare at me, Challenge etched over his pale, chuboy face. We shake hands and he tries to crush my fingers; I adjust my grip slightly and within seconds, Pain flashes across those now Childish eyes.

"Have you heard from him recently?" I ask; I don't bother keeping Contempt from my tone, but there is a level cf Maturity that I find... surprising.

"He left the State... as you suggested."

Try **DEMANDED**; Abuse is Abuse; she tried to cover the bruises with Excuses: Rough Sex; as the CHILD of a Single Black Mother who went through an abusive Relationship, I **know** the Signs all too well. It is difficult to hide anything from a concerned Child, let alone one as intelligent and inquisitive as myself. I gave Bret a Choice: Leave her alone **forever...** or I'd tear his Soul, screaming, from his body and turn him into a Zombie. I nod grimly as I turn over the Idea of making **sure** he kept to his end of the Deal.

"Sir? I never thanked you." I smile, shaking my head.

Sasha points to me.

"**THAT** is Why, Desmond; you never take credit for the Good you do. I know everyone calls you Demon, but to me... with me, you have only been One Good Man."

"With a shitload of issues."

"Just like everyone else, Sir."

"And that Night?"

* * * *

"Her Loyalty to you..." Rachel pauses, staring at the glass of merlot she swirls in her hand.

* * * *

I sat in this very chair That Night: the Night Amy left, a curt email her Final Words. That Night everything within me exploded. Sasha dropped by for After-Hours, eager to Vent about another crappy shift Serving. I swallowed everything again and Listened; she stopped...

"What's Wrong?"

My neck twitched; I gripped the arm rest; breathing through my nostrils felt like...

Like the Beast; Feast on her Soul; she can withstand the Pain. YOU only Fear the SOURCE.

"Does m'Lord still have Talon Scream?"

"Yes..."

That Night I tore at her Soul; bound in many positions, **I Vented**; That Night I was little more than Bret: a frightened Kid who'd just been Abandoned; Angry at everything and no one; That Night I marked my Friend and Packmate **ONCE AGAIN!!!** That Night... I was Nothing.

And afterwards, Cold in the Sauce, I

released her from the straps on my bed without fanfare, turned to my desk when she was Free and in a strained whisper, Commanded her to leave. I expected her sobs to continue as she left. I expected everything... except for My Friend... **to Challenge Me.**

"I will endure much for a Good Man."

"It will be the Death of you."

"Gotta Die somehow." Silence.

"I expected more from you, Sir; I cannot Feel your Pain."

Not sorrow: **CHALLENGE.** Sasha rose; I turned, and when I saw the sad amusement as she flippantly brushed her shoulders off...

* * * *

"It worries me."

"I know." Rachel darts her gaze towards me; I **FEEL** it, but I don't actually see her gaze. I interlace my fingers, thumbs and forefinger forming Fire, the forefingers resting on my upper lip as my eyes Follow the ebb and flow within my Mind. After several seconds of silence I sigh, saying, "I'll deal with that after you leave." I frown ever so slightly, sensing that I forgot to Address her rambling around the outer edges of Thought as I slice the last of my steak into two pieces. "Worried she's misguided?" I watch Rachel smile, shrugging as her **own** decisions waft over her beautiful face; she blushes.

"It is... a possibility." She takes a carefully measured sip, though it doesn't conceal what I already know.

* * * *

"You're being foolish, Sasha."

"I know; I also know I'm right to be foolish...
at least with you, Sir."

I turn my head towards her, pausing for
several moments before completing the
maneuver.

"I will consider everything you've told me.
As Punishment for betraying your sister, you
will leave this place tonight; when I Require you
I will Summon you." She nods once, rising
slowly.

"Hoi!" I say as she reaches for the
doorknob. Sasha freezes, but doesn't turn, not
even when I allow silence to bloat the air.
Finally I ask, "Your Rents ever find out about
us?" A chuckle bursts from her.

"Grams. I had issues sitting down. She
asked; I told her the Truth; she got mad that I
blamed it on a Black Guy!!" I laugh.

"My Little One is All Grown Up now; be

Ready."

* * * *

"Why did she just leave?"

I pour water over Rachel's shoulder, watching with curious admiration as the clear fluid Obeys the curve of her flesh.

"Something I needed done, Dearest Rachel; enough about her. No Thoughts." I plant one faint kiss upon her shoulder, drawn in by the Scent. "You are leaving this Town."

"Yes, and you need not be saddened or worried; I've got a few contacts back Home still, and even with this Recession: Rich Folk gonna Eat and Bling in the Big Easy." She joins my chuckle, turning her head towards me; I drag my scruffy check against her cheek.

"Shave?"

As I sit on the closed toilet seat, a twisted snort-chuckle coils my lips into a smirk/smile; she is not the First I've allowed with Steele on My Neck. As she carefully and skillfully shapes my goatee, my Thoughts settle; though they are not on the beautiful Woman who Truly Loves me... Lady Rachel. Nor are they lingering around Sasha; not **even Amy** strayed from Memory. Not calm; the Moment seems to coalesce from individual snap-shots: Rachel commenting that I look too boyish without the goatee, the way her eyes slid over my neck as she examined her Work; when she runs her fingers over stubble, then smooth, water-slick flesh...

* * * *

There is a Moment: when the Mind makes a Connection and Understanding Blinds. It is a Powerful Moment, and many falter here. This is Why: they Step Back.

While it is Proper to Dig In, to brace oneself against the onslaught of Knowledge and

Wisdom as they overwhelm the Mind simultaneously, **NEVER STEP BACK. ONLY PUSH FORWARD!!!**

* * * *

I shudder, Focus on Rachel and allow myself to fall into her; sweeping her into my arms, I imagine Pouring my Emotions about her into Making Love. That I accomplish this...

If you Know a Thing to be True and Good, there is little need in Denying it; I Love Lady Rachel... and always will.

BACK TO REALITY

Rachel... gone a full thirty minutes. I Lurk
on Facebook, dark grumbling rumbles softly
through the base of my spine. I flip through a
few open documents, but nothing starts the
Creative Juices flowing... and at that Moment I
Understand: **Real Life** is knockin' at the Door;
and thrice-damn... as if on cue...

*Yo Demon; I Know you're Watchin'; need
ya tomorrow; had an Issue.* Chef; I don't need
a Time: **I work Vampire Hours.** I don't reply,
simply snatch up my Smart Phone: Back to the
Grind, ya 'eard me?

"Yo Kilo; what the fuck went down yo?"

"**MAAAaaaaannn...**" Looks like Chef's
shit-fucked; based on **THAT** I ain't *about* to

walk into that place: Fuck-Up my **natural**
High!!

"Yo." Oh, shit; felt my gut go cold.

"He hit Amy, D."

"He picked his Time; knew I wasn't gonna
set foot there." You'd have to rewind Time to
hear the unholy Silence, marked Street
Poetically by Biggie Smalls' *Warning* bumpin'
the air.

"Yeah."

Now... if the place were more like Home I'd
be Gone for a Minute; the only thing that kept
him **alive** is Amy.

"Did I come up?" More unholy silence; I
shook my head, sighing as I Realized I could no
longer see Rachel's Face... **FEEL** anything I
Felt during her stay.

"Don't Call Me on this; I can't get back On Paper, D."

"Solid; keep ya head down, ya 'eard?"

Ten seconds later: Sasha sends this: *He's baiting you; got a crew waiting.*

I don't even give a shit what started this; all I want...; I spit: venomous laughter. Amy's Baby Daddy probably thinks I'm solo; one phone call later and the only thing I know: the Night will Bleed. I blaze, throw on some pure Big Easy Thug-on-Patrol and Zone until Nightfall.

And **right** as my Ride drives up... ***there is AMY... BABY IN TOW!!!***

"You can't kill him."

"Why?"

"I Love him; kill him and you kill a part of me." She isn't begging: *she is trying HARD to reach something within me. SHE'S* ***TERRIFIED!!!***

I stare at her for some time... *trying to figure out if she'd Snitch me out for Flat-Linin' his sorry ass.* I'm not concerned about her brat: non-issue... unless I kill **her**; raising another man's kid after killing him **does** bring the most deliciously sadistic Torment to my Mind, and I Imagine its Stain on my Soul while Amy's face falls little by little.

"Please, Desmond. Give Me Your Word." Driver racks the sawed-off; I snarl in agreement.

"**DON'T**; not after you left me Cold in the Sauce, bitch."

"I'll **deal** with him. **PLEASE...** Your Word." **NOW** she Begs... ***PROPERLY.***

The Maiden and The Demon

An Urban Gothic Romance

As if the Reason for begging isn't Selfish...

"Make it quick; Motivate." I'm inside the all-black SUV, surrounded by Gutta and Strange Clouds, the Night my dark Shadows to bounce through; the blunt is in rotation and Bullshit joins Rap Lyrics as narrowed eyes pierce the dark.

Bitch ain't even a Memory; Bad Sign.

* * * *

"He's at your Workplace; Amy *tracked* him there." I glance at my cell; the expected message is brief:

Hail Mary

"Let's Ride."

* * * *

Lord

Forgive me for the

Shit

I've gotta do

Just to See

Another Glorious Day

In Your Sight.

(((Lie of the Repentant Thug))

* * * *

"What's up?"

"Drive. Right now your Mission is to Talk me Down."

"Why? Who pissed you off?" The glare is long, slow and unspeakably Unholy in its frozen, inhuman emotionless.

"AH...; been waitin' for this; got Single Malt in-flop I take it."

"Here: hit dis and Drive, Dallas." I secure my seat belt before flicking my gaze through this windshield.

* * * *

"Wanna know what I think... *honestly?*"

"Shoot; you know me and the Rules here."

"Why you bein' such a **BITCH?**"

"Run it by me." Dallas raises the rocks glass held in true Pimp Fashion as he prepares to Pontificate.

"When I first met you, you *ran* them Hoes!!! Had everyone straight **shook!!!** Then you got involved with that one...." I nod as I watch his expressions Speak Thoughts that cannot be contained by Words. **Street Thoughts: I Changed... and not in a Good Way.**

"Trying **hard** to change my Old Ways, ya 'eard me? Tryin' **HARD.**"

From the look and laugh, I Knew; the Effort wasn't a total loss, but if I continued to allow Thoughts of Amy to infest my Mind and **SOUL...**

Bitch-Azz-Nigga... *ready to Fuck-Up the Game!!!* I nod quietly, pondering the Reality before me as Dallas takes a casual sip, eyes Pimp-to-the-Sky as if he doesn't have a care in the world: just watching Enlightenment Dawn.

"Damn," I sigh.

"When did you two Hook Up anyhow... **and HOW???**" He adjusts the ever-present Dallas Cowboys baseball cap before adding his rocks glass to my cluttered computer desk.

I shrug. "I finally decided to open up to someone about the stuff I'd been writing; you know I came through Those Waters, right?" Dallas nods, a cruel grin splitting his graying goatee as he reaches for his pack of Newports: instinct; he remembers the cigar after finding it during his lighter self-pat-down.

"And that was her IN; you let her get *too* close; right now, you're mad. Rightly so; she ain't said shit to you. Cut you off even as a Friend."

"**And that's HOW I intended this shit to...**" Dallas raises one hand, pulling back slightly.

"She was *looking* for Outside Action; played with your Heart and when you got too close..." Bolted; how many times had I SEEN that Scam run on Johns in clubs back home in the Big Sleazy?

"Fuck. Spike said the same thing, only he was nicer."

"He ya Boy; me... Imma tell ya like Pimp: You **need** to Harden your Heart again; got SOFT fuckin' wi' that one. Let 'er get *too close.*"

"Looking for love." Dallas frowns up, humming his displeasure.

"Stop that shit. You're getting older and ain't got the **TIME** for Lovey-Dovey shit: gotta make Dat Paper. And... why the fuck are you checking your Facebook?"

"She's got eyeballs watching me," I say softly. There's something in my Tone that catches my Attention as Dallas chimes in.

"Nice: fuck 'em; stop. Look. She got too close, **but YOU** got *way* too close. That's why she's got eyeballs on you. She don't wanna loose sight of you, and if this Book of yours takes off..."

"Been neglectng it and the others." I chew nothing, working my jaw as I struggle to Feel the Words clearly in my Mind.

"**Neglecting Yo Money.**" I turn smoothly. Dallas puffs on the expensive cigar, a Gift for his Services this Evening.

"Pimp Sin Two."

"What's the First?"

"Trustin' a Ho," I chuckle.

"**TRUE!!!**"

And the First tends to lead to the Second.

* * * *

"Been silent, D; Thinking. Good Sign."

"Thinking about something that's been buggin' me all day; I'm screwin' myself over on Serious Biz because of her... letting Emotions dictate Actions."

"Cold. **NOW** ya thinkin' Pimp... but ya still angry with her."

"She abandoned me... cut me off... Silence; like ya said: Too Close. Got issues with being cut off for... who knows Why. And if I ask..." I feel the snarl. Dallas picks up my glass bowl and takes an exaggerated pull, *knowing* I'll make some smart-ass comment: busting the Rage.

"Why don't you Put her on Blast like Freddy did Ailene?"

"Two Reasons: I try to keep **some** of Who I Am outta my shit; the second comes from some shit I've encountered before."

"What?' **NOW** he is interested: a Tale from The Demon's past!!!

"Usual day back home: just before Work; Power-Cached a dime bag..."

"Pothead!"

"... and whipped up my **only** Incest Story **to DATE!!!** When I came back home to check my responses... got one; seems she'd had the exact experience... *down to the detail!!!* And when I say Details: **I got the NAMES RIGHT!!!!**"

"Did you know her?" he asks, those expressive orbs wide with amazement.

"Nope: just a Story I whipped out while baked... just before going to work. I remember... it put me in a good mood to know I'd stretched my twisted Mind into something forbidden. Of course... there's a seriously fucked-up aspect to that story: the guy had a Sexual condition: he could only last 420 Seconds!!!"

"Bullshit."

I show him the email.

* * * *

"So. Who's next?"

"Too soon." Lie.

"Bullshit; you've already got a few lined up..."

"Going *there* means going back to my old Ways." True enough; I see a particular image in my Mind; it brings warm memories of Slummin' through the French Quarter for no damned reason.

"Like..."

"Runnin' Hoes."

"Problem?" I flash Dallas a devilish grin.

"Look... most of 'em don't want Relationships, and you **really** don't want or **NEED** one right now. Find one. Fuck 'em... but *get paid in the Process!!!* Then... when you're done... leave."

"No Diseases. No babies. No Drama."

"Aw... *expect* the **DRAMA** Demon: all they wanna do is Play with Emotions and have theirs Played with. Game. Simple." He puffs arrogantly on the cigar, **PROUD** of the dark wisdom offered.

"Just like that." Dallas nods, his face returning to Serious School.

"If you LET this... everything: GONE. I know you: Money pisses you off. So? Forget the Money... what about your Writings... and that Dream of yours? Gone?"

Fading: **FAST**. Already I'd trashed several Stories because they degenerated into blind, emotion-drenched Rants. Worse are the carefully constructed philosophical Flows that snarl up, tangled into inconceivable wire-mesh mess.

"Be a shitload easier if I were back Home; hit Cocaine Corner, Slot-and-Run with a skeezy Skripper-Ho; Bounce to Da Crib... *eventually...* and Call it a Night." I snort a chuckle, shaking my head at memories I consider Warm-Fuzzy and Dangerous. 'Felt more at Home dippin' through those Shadows than I do here."

"You stopped to Smell the Roses and got Stung by a bee; somethin' my Mom told me when I was sixteen I think... **last** time I ever let a bitch Get That Close." From his expression, I figure Dallas doesn't buy that bullshit; sounds Proper for the Moment.

"I'm going back home. It will take Time. **MONEY**, naturally, but *TIME* is the real issue." I sigh as my Thought slowly uncurls.

"Lemme ask you somethin': back when you first came here, you'd tear a head off without..."

"Not without: *with...*; I was Angry, Confused and so damned Defensive I couldn't stand myself."

"Given; but **you were Pimp!!!** You never

let a pair of tits and a smile get in the way...
until she found a Way Inside." I nod. "Now..."

"Now... I'm Re-Focused."

"Don't sound..."

"Takes Time to push down that nagging
itch for Love; not **LONG** at this Rate."

"*THERE* he is!!!" Dallas nearly shouts, a
broad grin splitting his face as my brow furrows.

I take a hit: LONG and DEEP; I Dragon
Exhale, sit back and Think for several minutes;
the Hip Hop has us both Street-Noddin' as our
Drone erases Workplace Drama-Induced
Stress. My eyes narrow and open as Thoughts
collide: Waves upon Waves; I Float on and in
the water, Seeing and Knowing. I pour another
shot: Dallas, still nursing his Three-Fingers,
jerks in surprise.

"MORE?"

"Gonna Write tonight; been neglectin' Biz."
DAMN does it Feel *GOOD* to have Thoughts
gearing up in my head... to **HEAR** the Stories
once more. Dallas chuckles, and for once there
is genuine Happiness in his Tone and his body
Relaxes.

"So? Who. Is. Next?"

"I tend to Break my Toys," I chuckle Darkly,
amused... *and PLEASED.*

"That Bondage shit... Remember: ya GOT
a few." *More than you know, ya old Dog!!*

"Yeah... **but I'm not sure I wanna put in
the Effort to Properly Train a Slut.**" That
always leaves a mess in the end; Messes and
Burning Bridges: not Good-for-Biz. Regular **or**
Personal. *Except for Sasha-Bushi...*

"Got somethin' better to fill ya Time Card?" I sit back and sigh, resting my left hand over my goatee as I Ponder my Reply.

"You mean outside of the other Books and other Money items, getting back Home? No." I sigh heavily. "Not that I foresee. Not Looking for Love; ready for the shit-storm, though. Don't like braggin', but Tender-and-Loving I ain't. Not now." Maybe not ever; **that** is the Cold emptiness in my chest. Dallas swirls the Last Swig, smiling gently.

"Then Make dat Money." I sigh, smiling, a bit sadly, but full of Focus and pleasant Street coldness. I raise my glass in Toast.

"Ball 'til ya Fall, ya 'eard."

* * * *

Epilogue:

An Urban Gothic Romance

"I used to have a heart; not sure when, but somewhere along this Journey called Life it got ripped from my chest and utterly destroyed, left to rot in the red clay. I picked up what was left, cleaned it as best I could; then I carefully concealed what was left in the deepest, darkest pit of Oblivion, surrounded by savage, unholy Creatures.

I don't Flash or Bling; I prefer to dress casually: jogging pants, denim jeans, loose fitting shirts; because of this I am considered unfit by most Females I encounter. Unfit because I don't have the cred flow to support the Live-Outside-My-Means lifestyle that is the Norm. I have an ancient Work Ethic, meaning I believe Hard Work isn't something to be shunned or relegated to poor, uneducated breeders; I'm proud of my Career Choice: Culinary. I Craft Tales in my spare time, putting my ever-thinking Mind to use; but it hasn't made me filthy rich, so I'm not acceptable to Normal Society, especially the Females.

*I'm not accepted for **many** Reasons/Excuses; I won't let Females talk to me like I'm some child to be scolded or the next Penis-wielding Paycheck they have yet to* *fleece. I'm not Money Hungry, willing and* **eager** *to fuck over everyone,* **including** **Family***, just for a few dollars more. Paranoid from birth, I'm not a pill popper; I blaze up when I'm stressed instead of hitting the bar to flirt with whatever rancid twat happens to be available. When I look around my doss, I see a place I once called Home; it looks Lived-In, as if* **HUMAN BEINGS** *existed, laughed and* **loved** *within the simple Four Walls. It isn't a castle; I didn't have servants rushing to keep pace with my eccentric Orders, cowering before me as I dole or chump-change scraps for them to scrape by with; been broke damn near my entire Life, so I know what has Value and what doesn't.*

I'm a Lost Soul refusing to give up on True Love; Fool by Normal Standards. By Normal Standards I need to have a Bad Bitch bouncing off my dick and a **new** *one ready when I bore of that whore. I need serious bling and fat whips.*

Doesn't go that way... not for me; I look Within the Flesh-Form; always have; in the end, **that** *is the Person you sleep with, hold tightly,* **LOVE!!!** *But I'm a fool for separating Love from Money; I'm an idiot for wanting Love to outlast the cred flow. And for this... I find myself alone,*

abandoned *even by those who claim to still love and care for me...* **all because I'm Hustling Legit and ain't Paid-in-Full-Times-Ten.**

So, if you follow this line of bullshit, the instant I start making money from my Legal Hustle, Love should be mine. Hey... forgive me for Knowing a bit about money-hungry Hoes: that dog won't Hunt; once I'm Paid, they'll **only** *look at my wallet, giving my clothes the once-over first, just to make sure I can afford their Ho ass.*

Here is how shit will shake out: if you won't Walk with me at my lowest point... if all you ever had for me were false smiles, silence, slams and insults, do **not** *expect me to suddenly become the Prince of Stupid and start acting like anything other than the hard working paranoid fucker who lost everything, and with only himself and God, got back up. Don't expect a handout; I wasn't given Jack Shit; expect the same ruthless fucker who was left to wallow in whatever pit of ooze God laid out. Expect the same heartless bastard who comes in to work, knocks out his shift and bounces; expect the same Drive, determination and* *utterly evil Mentality: Honor, Honesty, Loyalty and Duty **BEFORE** Money. **AND DO NOT LOOK FOR LOVE WITHIN THIS FLESHFORM; LOST THAT ALONG MY JOURNEY, THANKS TO BEING FOOLISH ENOUGH TO DARE HOPE SOMEONE OUT THERE HAS ENOUGH ROOM IN THEIR EXISTENCE FOR ME.***

All I have is Nothing; that will do."

Rachel frowns, the expression cute... not to mention slightly confused; after reading, she chuckles softly, her right hand reflexively caressing her belly.

"One day, I'll tell you about your Father." She closes the document with one mouse-click. "It's a strange tale."

CREDITS

Cover Art: Kenneth Strader

Back Cover Photo: © Melissa Christina
Photography; visit her at
www.melissachristinaphotograhpy.zenfolio.com

This Book owes much to Katrina Walker:
former High School Classmate and Editor.